hinker's Invisible Wings

101 Chinese-English bilingual poems

Written or translated by Yiyan HAN

思想者的隱形翅膀

漢英雙語詩歌 101 首

韓亦言 著譯

序言

靈感一直是詩的獵奇。

就像一隻金輪蜘蛛
詩人經由現實的散沙
一路翻尋到達丘頂
那是想像力女神的領地
嗜蛛蜂為女神排卵。
卵在它的背上
像詩詞一樣地孵化。

筋疲力盡的詩人
容易成為嗜蛛蜂的獵物。
於是他捲成一個金輪
以驚人的速度
從丘頂滾下。
一串又一串的詩行
留在了沙坡上。

《思想者的隱形翅膀》
這本書正是亦言出色的獵奇。

埃爾韋·德勒
比利時作家和詩人

說明：德勒先生出版了諸多的文學作品與詩集，同時也獲得了多種獎項。

註：
• 金輪蜘蛛，golden wheel spider（Carparachne），見於納米比亞沙漠。
• 嗜蛛蜂，spider hunting wasp（Pompilidae），以蜘蛛為食。

Foreword

Poetry is hunting for inspiration.

A poet as a Carparachne
plows through the loose sands of reality
to the top of the hill
where the goddess of the imagination reigns
and the wasp lays on behalf of the goddess.
Her eggs on his back
will hatch like verses.

Totally exhausted is the poet
one easy prey for the Pompilidae.
he curls into a ball
and rolls off the sand dune
at a breakneck speed.
What follows down
is poetry.

Thinker's Invisible Wings shows
Yiyan is an excellent hunter.

HERVE DELEU
Belgian author and poet

HERVE DELEU
Belgian author and poet

Published books

- De Vissende Hond 2017 - Roman
- Avalanche 2018 - Roman
- Het Blad 2019 - Roman
- Amy 2021 – Roman

Honors list of poetry 2012-2022

- 1st prices Belgium (Kessel-Lo /Opwijk (2x) / Ronse / Gavere / Brussel (2x) / Berlare / Lissewege)
- 1st prices The Netherlands (Rotterdam / Haarlem / Angerlo-Doesburg / Valkenburg / Amsterdam)
- 1st price United States (CosmoFunnel LA)

Awards list of poetry 2012-2022

- Lofdichter Gentse Feesten (Belgium)
- Gastdichter Oostduinkerke (Belgium)
- Dichter van Gavere (Belgium)
- Huisdichter Monique Neyzen (Spain)
- Eredichter Namibië (South-Afrika)

前言

作為一名擁有博士學位的曾經的科學研究者居然要出版一本自己的詩集，心中自然是誠惶誠恐的。人的一生，總是要不斷地學習與進步，這本詩集就是我學習寫作的一個結果。這裡收集的 101 首漢英雙語詩歌，大多數發表在「大紀元」、「希望之聲」和「看中國」等網站；有些英文詩歌自我發表在一些英文詩歌平臺，擁有一定數量的英語讀者。

所有的詩歌，無論是自己創作的還是翻譯的，都是我自己挑選並且喜歡的。儘管本人的能力有限，但都是盡心盡力完成的作品，期待讀者也能夠喜歡。書中的詩歌大致分為四章：情感、生活與生命、社會以及思與想。

美國哲學家—科學家與唯靈論者約瑟夫·亞歷山大·薩多尼説過：「一首好詩不過是思想者之歌的旋律：而文字就是他夢想的種子。」假如讀者可以從我的詩中拾起一二顆這樣的種子，本人就感到欣慰了。

韓亦言 於英國
2023 年 4 月 8 日

Preface

As a former scientific researcher with a PhD, I'm naturally apprehensive about publishing a collection of my own poems. Since my life is always about continuous learning and trying to better myself, this anthology is a result of my learning to write. Most of the 101 Chinese-English bilingual poems in this collection have been published on websites such as the Epoch Times (Chinese) and Sound of Hope; Some English poems are self-published on some English platforms for poetry, and have a certain number of English readers.

All the poems, whether my own writing or translation, are selected and liked by myself. I've done my best to complete each piece, though my ability might be limited, and I hope readers will like them too. The poems are roughly divided into four chapters: Emotions, Life, Society, and Think and Reflect.

The US philosopher-scientist and spiritualist Joseph Alexander Sadony once said: "A GOOD POEM is but the melody of a thinker's song: the words, the seed of his dream." I'd be gratified if readers could find one or two such seeds in my poems.

Yiyan Han
England, UK
April 6, 2023

目錄

Contents

Chapter 2 ❖ Life · 87

Chapter 3 ❖ Society ·······················161

Chapter 4 ❖ Thought · 225

情 感
Emotions

我表了白，我表了白
　　對我愛的人表了白
　　　　我顫冷發抖、驚恐萬狀

I told my love, I told my love
　　I told her all my heart
　　　　Trembling, cold, in ghastly fears

至 愛

英國 伊莉莎白·巴雷特·白朗寧（1806－1861）

如何愛你
我來細數愛的方式
我愛你 至高至廣至深 至我魂所及
如冥冥之中 乞求至高無上的完美和上帝
我愛你 就像每日心靈深處之需
在陽光下 在燭火旁 永不停止
我愛你 無拘無束 如同追求正義
我愛你 純潔無比 就像在唱讚美詩
我愛你 以我的童真 帶着昔日悲痛的激情
我愛你 以我的愛 她似曾消失
以我的愛 她曾經獻給失去了的天使 ─
我愛你 用我的呼吸 微笑 眼淚 以及整個生命
─ 還有 如果上帝允許
我將在天國愛你 更深地愛你

註：標題「至愛」為譯者所加，作者常被華人稱為「白朗寧夫人」。

Sonnet XLIII

Elizabeth Barrett Browning (1806 – 1861)

How do I love thee? Let me count the ways.
I love thee to the depth and breadth and height
My soul can reach, when feeling out of sight
For the ends of being and ideal grace.
I love thee to the level of every day's
Most quiet need, by sun and candle-light.
I love thee freely, as men strive for right.
I love thee purely, as they turn from praise.
I love thee with the passion put to use
In my old griefs, and with my childhood's faith.
I love thee with a love I seemed to lose
With my lost saints. I love thee with the breath,
Smiles, tears, of all my life; and, if God choose,
I shall but love thee better after death.

落花的詠嘆

落花春去：
怒放時展示美麗；謝幕時回歸大地
這猶如逝去的青春

莎士比亞説：
「粗野的風，總想吹落五月迷人的花蕾」(1)
是啊，粗野的風一定是嫉妒花的美麗

而今我見落花：
想到那年那月那日天安門廣場上的青年們
不禁自問：我的熱血有沒有往日的溫度？

1919 年 5 月 4 日為標記的《五四運動》(2)
文化的還是政治的？啓蒙或是救亡？
一百年之後依然眾説紛紜

70 年後的 1989 年 6 月 4 日 (3)
又是年輕的學生們又是天安門廣場
這一次，歷史還年輕而且世界看得見

五四 30 年後，中共叛亂成功禍害大陸
六四 30 年後，中共物質與思想病毒遍及全球
中國要忍受多久？世界要容忍多久？

從近代史，看清中共法西斯 (4)
世界正在巨變，昏睡的應該甦醒
站著而不是平躺，站著才能擁抱自由的陽光

註：

(1) 莎士比亞的十四行詩：《永恆的青春》
　　http://www.epochtimes.com/b5/20/12/5/n12598088.htm

(2) https://zh.wikipedia.org/zh-tw/ 五四運動

(3) https://zh.wikipedia.org/zh-tw/ 六四事件

(4) 《世紀大瘟疫中的思考》
　　https://www.secretchina.com/news/b5/2021/02/02/961202.html

Aria of Fallen Petals

Petals were fallen and the spring's gone:
Exhibiting beauty when in full bloom
Returning to the earth after a curtain call
Like a lost youth of all

In Shakespeare's *Sonnet XVIII*:
"Rough winds do shake the darling buds of May"
O alas! the rough northerly wind
Is jealous of the beauty of the darling buds

Now I see the fallen petals:
Come back the fallen youth in the Tian-an-men Square
I can't help but ask myself:
Does my blood have the same temperature as before?

May 4, 1919, marked as the May 4th Movement
Was it a cultural or political?
Or an enlightenment or a self salvation?
Opinions still differ after a hundred more years

June 4, 1989, seventy years later
It's young students again
and it's in the Tian-an-men Square again
This time, history is young and the world has seen!

Thirty years after the May 4th, the CCP's rebellion
Succeeded to has brought disaster to China
Thirty years after the June 4th, the CCP's ideological viruses
Has been spread all over the world, so has its Wuhan virus!
How long will the Chinese have to suffer,
and the world to tolerate it?

Learning from the modern history
We should see the evil nature of the CCP fascist
The world is changing dramatically, wake up if still asleep
Stand up rather than lie down flat
Only stand up can we embrace the sunshine of freedom

民國夢

民國夢　是共和夢
一九一二年一月一日
這一天成就了亞洲第一共和
民國夢　是民主夢
走過了艱難　夢已成真
民國夢　是自由夢
如今　民主進步 —
淚水轉換成笑容 (1)

民國的臺灣人　是自由人
民國的臺灣人　是民主人
民國的火炬　點亮了臺灣　照亮著對岸
更點亮了每一顆追求自由的心
這火炬　與歐美自由女神手擎的一樣
點亮了理想　也點亮了希望

民主制度的力量
勝過船堅炮利　更勝過萬馬千軍
勝過地大物博　更勝過人口眾多
這巨變的大時代
呼喚博大胸懷　呼喚勇敢堅強
更呼喚人性謙卑

悠悠中華　幾千年上下承傳
長江黃河　滔滔不絕奔大海
華夏子民　心懷若谷兼納百川
民國夢　豈可安睡在綠島
共和夢　早就該破鏡重圓
民主自由　在追求的路上
讓我們肩並肩　手挽手
雲厚霧密時　豎起太陽花
日酷雨冷時　撐起傘一把

註：

(1) 蔡英文：淚水轉換成笑容
https://www.setn.com/News.aspx?NewsID=118960

Dream of the Republic

The dream of the Republic of China
Is the dream of a country of republic. January 1, 1912
The first republic in Asia established on this day
The dream of the Republic of China is a dream of democracy
Through difficult challenges, this dream has now come true
The dream of the Republic of China is a dream of freedom
The democracy today is in progress —
Tears have turned into smiles [1]

Taiwanese in the Republic are the people of free
Taiwanese in the Republic are the people of democracy
The torch of the Republic has lit up the isles of Taiwan
Illuminated the land across the strait, and also lit up
The heart of each freedom pursuer
This torch is the same as the one held by the Statue of Liberty
In Europe and America, which lights up the ideas
Also lights up the hope

The power of a democratic system
Is stronger than the big warship with guns
Surpasses thousands of troops with strong artillery
Is better than a large land with good resources
And a large population. This great era of great changes
Call for open minds, call for bravery and strength
And call for humanity and humility

The history of China has been passed down for thousands of years
The Yellow River and Yangtze always surge towards the sea
The people of Hua Xia must be open-minded with a big heart [2]
How could the dream of Republic only stay in the green island?
The shattered mirror of Republic should be put back together
Freedom and democracy are already on the road of pursuing
let's stand arm in arm, and shoulder to shoulder
When the clouds and fog are thick and dark, sunflowers stand up [3]
When the sun is scorching and the rain icy, umbrellas are handy [4]

Footnote:
1. Tears have turned into smiles, a speech by Tsai Ing-wen after winning the general election on January 16, 2016.
2. Hua Xia, an ancient name for China.
3. The Taiwan Sunflower Movement between March 18 and April 1 2014.
4. The Hong Kong Umbrella Movement, started from September 26, 2014 and in later years.

江城子 · 乙卯正月二十日夜記夢

蘇軾 於 1075 年

十年生死兩茫茫，不思量，自難忘。
千里孤墳，無處話淒涼。
縱使相逢應不識，塵滿面，鬢如霜。

夜來幽夢忽還鄉，小軒窗，正梳妝。
相顧無言，惟有淚千行。
料得年年腸斷處，明月夜，短松岡。

Dream Recall

— Love was when loved each other

SU Shi

Ten years since thou passed away, in my memory thou forever stay,
though avoiding thinking of thee. The worlds of life'n'death separate us.
As thy lonely tomb is thousand miles away,
to whom could I express my grief and misery?
Wouldn't recognise each other even if we met,
with our dusty faces, and hairs turned grey from black.

I dreamt of back to our home town, saw thee sit
facing the small window and dressing up.
We were staring at each other without words,
only with tears gushing out from our eyes.
Imagine thou would be bitterly weeping and longing for me,
year after year, in a moonlit night, on the deserted ridge of pine shrubs.

Footnote:

SU Shi (蘇軾 , 1037 – 1101) , a great poet in Song Dynasty, wrote this poem in 1075 to commemorate his beloved wife who died 10 years earlier. I translate this great piece into English in an attempt to show that love is eternal. A great poem lives forever ever. The subtitle is added by the translator.

那個眨眼的瞬間

美國 羅茜曼妮·娟 — 奧斯廷

昨天夜裡　我見到了你
就在那一條沿河的街上
你瞅見我　我的眼睛
也看著你的方向！

鎖在一起的　是你我的雙眼
你的眼睛異彩繽紛
呵　是街上的路燈
讓它放出絢麗的光芒！

儘管　你的誘人
嘴唇緊閉著　可你
動人的眼睛
說出萬語千言……！

那是一個完美的夜晚
天空　熠熠星光
你我　目光一對接
瞬間　就奪走了我的心！

呵　在那樣迷人的時刻
你我的心　熱切地渴望
美美的一個吻
萬般戀欲的井噴
就在那個一眨眼的瞬間！

你的感情　是那樣的強和烈
你的秋波　激盪我的心潮澎和湃
你我　雙雙墜入情海
這種莫名的衝動
就在那個一眨眼的瞬間！

你我　這次的相遇是緣
命中註定　不可避免
呵　情感的大潮
緊緊地擁抱著你我
向神祕莫測的盡頭沖去！

Just A Wink Of An Eye

Rose Marie Juan-Austin

Last night I saw you
On the waterfront
You glanced at me
And I looked your way!

Our eyes locked together
And your eyes shifted colors
As they caught the light
Installed at the waterfront!

Though your alluring lips
Were sealed
Yet those lovely eyes spoke
A thousand words...!

The night was perfect
With star studded sky
You winked at me
And snatched my heart right away!

It was a wonderful moment
Our hearts craved for a kiss
With the bliss
Everything happened
In just a wink of an eye!

You were utterly crazy
Your glance made me crazy
We were both swept away
By this undefined ecstasy
In just a wink of an eye!

We soared the inevitable
We could not resist
The high tides of emotion
It knocked us down
To the very end!

春天的思念

說是在春天相見
那是一個美麗的夢境
封閉孤獨的日子　一天又一天
藏在心底的　久遠的思念
相隔千里的你我
相見的欲望　勝過萬語千言

說是在春天相見
那是一個遙遠的雪景
天邊的雪山上　銀色一片
滑雪板撐起美麗的綠紅
伴隨　株株雪松
這是期待中的　春天的夢

說是在春天相見
那是一生深情的想念
越過千山萬水　春夏秋冬
相距遙遠的你我　願望似一隻蝴蝶
帶著平安的信息　祝福叮嚀
乘著電波　飛到你的身邊

Longing For You in the Spring

Said to meet up in the spring
and it's a beautiful dream
The lockdown days were lonely long and dark
The thoughts long hidden in the bottom
of my heart suddenly come up
Though we're thousands of miles apart
the desire of seeing you is hard to describe

Said to meet up in the spring
and it's a distant snow scene
Above the snow-capped mountains afar
is a dreamy world of silver
The skis hold up the beauty in red and green
surrounded by snow-covered cedars
This is long-awaited, the dream in the spring

Said to meet up in the spring
and it's a longing of life time
Across thousands of mountains and waters
across winter, autumn, summer and spring
flies the butterfly of longing and good wishes
The messenger of peace, blessings and reminders
comes to your side, riding a wave of internet

細數我的情
—卓文君給司馬相如的回信，常稱為《數字詩》

一別之後，
二地相懸。
只說三、四月，
誰知五、六年。
七弦琴無心彈，
八行字無可傳。
九連環無故折斷，
十里長亭望眼欲穿。
百思念，
千掛牽，
萬般無奈把郎怨。

萬語千言說不完，
百無聊賴十倚欄。
重九登高孤身看孤雁，
八月中秋月圓人不圓。
七月半燒香秉燭問蒼天，
六月間心寒不敢搖蒲扇。
五月石榴似火，偏遇冷雨催花瓣；
四月枇杷未黃，我欲對鏡心煩亂。
急匆匆，三月桃花隨水轉；
飄零零，二月風箏線扯斷。
噫！郎君兮，盼只盼，
下一世你為女來，我為男！

註：標題和副標題為韓亦言所加。該版本見
https://www.aboluowang.com/2015/0227/520312.html

Love of Countless

ZHUO Wenjun

Being apart from the day *one*,
crave for each other in *two* distant places.
Promised only to live separately for *three* or *four* months,
but heaven knows it's already been for *five* to *six* years.
No mood to play my *seven*-string zither,
and to nowhere I can send my *eight*-line poems.
The *nine*-interconnected-rings shattered for no reason,
and look so eagerly afar through the *ten*-mile pavilion.
With *hundred* times of longing,
thousand times of worrying, I'm murmuring
to myself your name *ten-thousand* times, all but a helpless moaning.

Ten-thousand words and a *thousand* letters ain't enough to utter,
being bored *hundred* times and leaning *ten* times a day on baluster.
On the double-*nine* day, lonely on the hilltop,
stare at the lonely flying goose, [1]
and on the day of mid-*eighth* month, envy the round reunion moon,
alone on my own. [2]
Burning incense and holding candles, pray to the Heaven
on the day of mid-*seventh* month, [3]
and in the hot *sixth* month my heart is so cold
that I dare not wave the cattail leaf fan.
Pomegranate in the month *five* is red like flame,
but it's heartbroken to see its delicate petals are hit by cold rain;
In the *fourth* month loquat isn't yet yellow,
my turmoil heart refuses to look in the mirror.
Hustle and bustle, in the month *three* peach flowers spin in the river;
Wandering and drifting, the month *two* kite falls with a broken string.
O alas! My beloved husband, I do wish you'd be a woman
in the rebirth of our lives next-*one*, and me a man!

Footnote:

• This poem is often called *Poem of Numbers* in the Chinese literature, said by ZHUO Wenjun (卓文君) , a poetess in the Western Han Dynasty, ~200 BC. As the legend goes, it was a return letter to her husband, Sima Xiangru (司馬相如) who was a famous intellect and also a poet and then worked away from home as a government officer, after she received a cold letter from him. In his letter, he heartlessly wrote only a string of numbers from one to ten-thousand *without* the ending one-hundred-million (億), the biggest number at that time. "Without one-hundred-million" in the Chinese pronunciation, *wu-yi*, implies "no fancy or not interested". In other words, his letter hinted that he wanted to leave her. The story had a happy ending though. On receiving her poem, he felt so shameful that he rushed back home and took his wife with him. The couple stayed married and lived a good life ever after.

• All the months in this poem are lunar ones in the Chinese calendar. (1) *Double Ninth Festival*, September 9th, also known as *Double Yang Festival*, traditionally for worshipping ancestors, also climbing and hiking. (2) *Mid-Autumn Festival*, August 15th, also known as *Moon-cake Festival*, for family reunion. (3) *Ghost Festival*, July 15th, also known as *Hungry Ghost Festival*, traditionally for offering food to the deceased ancestors or other good spirits.

• The title "Love of Countless" is added by the translator to reflect the speaker's deepest love expressed for her husband.

情感 ❖ Emotions

梅花之戀

梅花 美麗的梅花
民國之花 我的國花
哪裡有土地
哪裡祢就開花
人人喜愛人人贊誇

梅花 自由的梅花
民國之花 我的國花
哪裡有人煙
哪裡祢就發芽
自由的人自由的家

梅花 堅韌的梅花
民國之花 我的國花
哪怕是嚴寒
哪怕風吹雨打
默默堅守默默開花

梅花 心中的梅花
民國之花 我的國花
母忘我在莒
把祢一直牽掛
無論海角無論天涯

梅花 英雄的梅花
民國之花 我的國花
如竹之不屈
如松一樣挺拔
青春不老青春煥發

作者心聲：
每到雙十，鄧麗君的《梅花頌》就會輕喚我心。民國，民國，自由的家園。希望
有作曲家譜曲，歌唱家吟唱。

Love You, the Winter-sweet

The blossom of winter-sweet, beautiful blossom
The flower of the Republic, of my country
Wherever the land is
You bloom freely
Everyone loves and praises you

The blossom of winter-sweet, tenacious blossom
The flower of the Republic, of my country
No matter if in bitter cold
No matter if in the icy rain and wind
You silently bloom and hold

The blossom of winter-sweet, hero's blossom
The flower of the Republic, of my country
Unbending like a bamboo
Vigorous as a cedar
Forever you're young and glow

The blossom of winter-sweet, blossom of free
The flower of the Republic, of my country
Wherever there's human
You grow freely
Land of free and man of free

The blossom of winter-sweet, blossom in my heart
The flower of the Republic, of my country
Never forget wherever you are
Long for you endlessly
No matter where I am on a day

愛的秘密

英國 威廉·布萊克 (1757-1827)

愛必須永遠珍藏在心底，
　　　愛從來不可表白；
愛如同微風輕拂
　　　無形而悄無聲息。

我表了白，對我愛的人表了白，
　　　我顫冷發抖、驚恐萬狀，
我向她傾訴了衷腸。
　　　唉！她真的離開！

她離開我之後不久，
　　　一位行者走過來，
無形而悄無聲息地將她帶走：
　　　留下了一聲嘆息。

Love's Secret

William Blake (1757-1827)

Never seek to tell thy love,
　　　Love that never told can be;
For the gentle wind doth move
　　　Silently, invisibly.

I told my love, I told my love,
　　　I told her all my heart,
Trembling, cold, in ghastly fears.
　　　Ah! she did depart!

Soon after she was gone from me,
　　　A traveller came by,
Silently, invisibly:
　　　He took her with a sigh.

夜晚約會

英國 羅勃特·白朗寧 (1812-1889)

灰色海面　黑色的長長海岸線
黃色半月　又大又低
沈睡的小小浪花　躍起
在驚嚇之中　翻騰不止
船頭一衝進那個海灣
我便踏上泥濘的沙灘

一英里暖暖的海邊　濃濃的海之味
穿過三塊田之後　一個農場在盡頭
窗格輕輕敲一下　火柴快快地一划
瞬間　噴發出藍色的火花
一個柔柔的聲音　驚喜與慌恐
兩顆心相擁　一起劇烈地跳動！

註：作者的妻子是伊莉莎白·巴雷特·白朗寧（Elizabeth Barrett Browning），
華人常稱之為白朗寧夫人。譯者也翻譯了一首她的詩「至愛」。

Meeting at Night

Robert Browning (1812-1889)

The grey sea and the long black land;
And the yellow half-moon large and low;
And the startled little waves that leap
In fiery ringlets from their sleep,
As I gain the cove with pushing prow,
And quench its speed i' the slushy sand.

Then a mile of warm sea-scented beach;
Three fields to cross till a farm appears;
A tap at the pane, the quick sharp scratch
And blue spurt of a lighted match,
And a voice less loud, thro' its joys and fears,
Than the two hearts beating each to each!

母 親

母親、親娘、媽媽
不同的稱呼，同樣的意思：
母親就是家
有母親就有不盡的思念
有母親就有無窮的牽掛

母親，平凡的母親
善良、堅韌、勤勞的媽媽
含辛茹苦一手將孩子撫養大
在艱難困苦的年頭
母親辛酸的眼淚
為她的孩子能否吃上飯而流
為了孩子有飯吃
她曾在嚴冬等在大河邊
希望能從過往的船上買些糧食
不識字的母親
盡全力支持孩子上學
期盼孩子有一個好的明天
孩子的命就是母親的命
她曾在半夜三更
背著腹痛的孩子走了幾里路求醫
當長大了的孩子離開了家
從那一刻起，孩子有了思念
無論在海角還是天涯
而孩子成了母親餘生的牽掛

當手機上傳來母親的呼喊：
兒啊，有空回家吧！
無奈的孩子只好大聲回答：
好、好、好。這其實是美麗的謊言，欺騙媽媽！
一天，手機上傳來了母親歸天的噩耗
無助的孩子再也無處說出安慰母親的話！
從此，離家的孩子成了孤兒
因為他沒有了母親、親娘、媽媽！
天堂的母親沒有了牽掛
離家的孩子只能在夢中回家！

Mother

Mother, mama, mum
Different ways to call but all the same
Mama means where the home is
When mum's at home
My longing never stops

Mother, ordinary mummy
Kind, forbearing and hard-working
Raised her children up single-handedly
Going through hardship in difficult years
Mother often shed her tears
Worrying about where the next dinner was
For children to have meals
She used to wait by the river in severe winter
Hoped to buy some grains from the passing boats
Mother was illiterate but encouraged
All her children to get educated in the hope
That they'd have a better future
She took care of the lives of all her children:
Once in the middle of the night
She carried one of her children who had an abdominal pain
And walked several miles to seek medical treatment
When children grew up and left home
From that moment on
Children were always in her worries
No matter where they were

When mum's voice came from the mobile:
Son, came home please when you were free!
Her helpless child had no choice but to answer loudly:
Yeah, yeah, yeah. This was a beautiful lie!
One day, the sad news of mum's death came from the mobile
That helpless child has since nowhere to comfort his mummy!
The children have become an adult-orphan from then on
Because they have no nowhere to call mother, mama, mum!
Mother's at heaven no longer with worries
And her survived children can only return home in their dreams!

母親的窯洞

—向高智晟先生偉大的母親致敬 (1)

窯洞　無論簡陋還是奢華
只要是母親一生的居所
她就是母親的化身　她就是母親

母親的窯洞裡有油燈
有黑暗　更多的時候是這樣
有歡聲笑語也有哭泣悲傷
有搖籃曲也有野狼嚎叫
有酒肉的香味也有臭豆腐味
炕上有大紅的棉被也有髒衫
可只要有母親在　窯洞就是天堂

窯洞裡跑出貍鼠和老兔子 (2)
也跑出狐狸和雞　雄雞啼明
窯洞才能起床　雙手捧著太陽
母親的窯洞裡裝得下整個宇宙
一粒黃土裡就有萬千世界

秦始皇和溥儀在窯洞裡笑談
划拳勸飲　陳勝吳廣送上桂花酒
袁世凱和毛澤東在洞外垂涎　膜拜
盤裡剩下的白骨　貍鼠的美餐
這就是母親的窯洞
自從盤古開天女媧補
后羿抹暗了九顆太陽

母親的淚讓黃河水清
讓長江水停　讓高山低頭
母親的淚是孩子的乳汁
是老佛爺的晨飲
是萬家燈火的油

母親的乳汁澆灌了田裡的油菜
也餵飽了狼溝裡走出來的紅狐 (3)
母親乾癟的胸懷　孕育了五湖四海
母親　從天上摘下星星給窯洞照明
也撈起水中的月亮

黃河之水從母親的子宮
一步千年　流進長江
沖向太平洋　母親的雙目白內障
在深藍色的海水裡看到宇宙中心
看到宇宙大爆發的一瞬
母親的眼睛裡只有藍天沒有陰霾

母親的窯洞是時光隧道
一秒繞地球七圈半　一瞬就是幾千年
一步從喜瑪拉雅到泰山
一步從青藏高原到阿爾卑士
母親的心臟跳動時就是火山呼吸
什麼時候噴發　無法預計
母親的血液流動時就是大海波浪
什麼時候沖上黃土高原　無法設想

母親在窯洞裡生下了一個國家
有時只生一個孩子　奶水將頭撐大
某個時候　母親生出了三皇五帝
更多的時候　生出地球的四分之一
不差一二個秦始皇帝

母親的大腳　巨無霸
走過萬水千山　留下愛情和怨恨
歡樂和悲傷　鮮花和毒草
母親也曾裹起了小腳
在窯洞裡寸步難行　離開洞門就迷路
這就是母親　這就是世界
怎麼描繪也不過分　只要塗料足夠
怎麼歌唱也不過分　只要五音俱全
怎麼書寫也不過分　只要是上帝的手筆(4)

母親的窯洞裡沒有跳躍
也沒有空白　窯洞一直在直白
窯洞裡偉人輩出　只要是生在
母親生前的窯洞　就可能是總統
沒有當總統的願望也不行
呵　生前的母親　盼望流浪的孩子
找到窯洞的燈火
呵　在天堂的母親　保佑失蹤的孩子
登上平安風順的路途

註：

(1) 「高智晟：我的平民母親」https://www.epochtimes.com/gb/5/3/18/n854721.htm

(2) 貍鼠：中共及其黨魁；老兔子：高智晟先生自稱。

(3) 紅狐，與貍鼠同一隱喻，泛指中共及其炮灰。

(4) 「高智晟：歷史是上帝的手筆」https://www.chinaaid.net/2017/08/blog-post_22.html

Mother's Cave

— Tribute to the great mother of Mr Gao Zhisheng [1]

Cave dwellings, no matter if simple or luxurious
So long as it's the residence of mother's lifetime
She is the embodiment of mother, and is the mother herself

In the mother's cave, there're oil lamps
But, more often, there's also darkness
There's laughter, as well as crying and sorrow
There're lullabies, as well as wolves' howling
It smells like wine and meat, as well as like stinky tofu
There're red cotton-padded quilts, as well as dirty shirts,
on the bed-stove
So long as mother lives in, the cave is like a heaven

The raccoon and the old rabbit come out [2]
of the cave, so do the fox and chicken
Only when a rooster crows, can you know it's time to get up
Not only holding the sun in her both hands
The mother's cave can hold the whole universe, as in Buddhism
There're tens thousands of worlds in a grain of loess

The first and last Emperors laughed and chatted in the cave
And one got the other to drink by a game of finger-guessing
While Chen Sheng and Wu Guang served them
with the osmanthus wine [3]
Yuan Shikai and Mao Zedong, outside the cave [4]
Were salivating, and worshipping on their bended knees
The bones left on their plates are delicious meals for the raccoons
This is the mother's cave, since Pangu created the heaven and earth
Nüwa amended the heaven's pillars and Yi shot down nine suns [5]

Mother's tears make the muddy water in the Yellow River clear
Stop the water flow in the Yangtze,
and let mountains to bow their heads
Mother's tears are the milk for children, the morning drink
of the Empress Dowager Cixi, and the oil of thousands of lamps

Mother's milk waters the rapeseed fields
Also feeds the red foxes that come out of a wolf ditch [6]
The mother's wizened breasts have also fed lakes and seas
Mother plucks stars from the sky to illuminate the cave
Also picks up the moon in the water

The water of the Yellow River from the mother's womb
Having crossed thousands of years
Flows into the Yangtze, and rushes to the Pacific
Mother's eyes of cataract, in a deep blue ocean
See clearly the centre of the universe and the moment
When the beginning of universe exploded
In mother's eyes, there is only blue sky without haze

Mother's cave is a time tunnel:
Seven and a half circles around the earth in just one second
and thousands of years in just a wink
From the Himalayas to Mt Tai, in just one step
So is from the Tibetan Plateau to Alps
When the mother's heart beats, it's like volcanic breathing
It's unpredictable when it will erupt
When the mother's blood flows, it's like the waves of sea
It's unimaginable when it will reach the Plateau of Loess

Mother, in the cave, has given birth to a nation
But sometimes to only one child, and the milk fills the big-heads
At certain time, mother gave birth to the rulers
Of Three Sovereigns and Five Emperors, yet more often
She gives birth to a quarter of population on the earth
Never short of one Emperor Qin, or two

Mother's big feet, of leviathan
Walk cross thousands of rivers and mountains
Leave behind love and resentment
Joy and sorrow, and flowers and weeds
Mother's feet were once bound with cloth
Inside the cave, hard to move even an inch
And she'll get lost if outside of the door
This is the mother, and this is the world
No matter how to paint it so long as there's enough ink
No matter how to sing it so long as the notes are hit
No matter how to write it
so long as following the God's handwriting [7]

There's no jump in the poem of mother's cave
Nor blank space in the realm of mother's cave
All is in a straightforward and plain language —
Great men are born in succession in caves
So long as it's the cave where mother lived
He might be an elected president even if no desire to be
O! Mother before her death was looking forward to
seeing her wandering child find the light of cave
O! Mother in heaven blesses her missing child
To trek and find a safe and smooth road

Footnote:
1. Gao Zhisheng: My Commoner Mother
   https://www.epochtimes.com/gb/5/3/18/n854721.htm
2. Raccoon: The CCP and its leaders and members; Old rabbit: Mr Gao Zhisheng calls himself.
3. The Chen Sheng and Wu Guang rebellion against the first Emperor Qin in 209-8 BC
4. Yuan Shikai (1859-1916), the first none-elected president of the Republic of China in 1912 after the Qing Dynasty, and soon died after he restored himself as an emperor in 1916. Mao Zedong (1893-1976), the de facto first emperor of the communist China.
5. Pangu, Nüwa and Yi, all regarded as "creators" of the heaven and earth according to some ancient Chinese myths.
6. The red fox, the same metaphor as the raccoon.
7. Gao Zhisheng: History is the handwriting of God
   https://www.chinaaid.net/2017/08/blog-post_22.html

故鄉的高原

蘇格蘭 羅伯特·伯恩斯 (1759 – 1796)

我的心留在那故鄉的高原兮，不在這裡，
我的心留在那高原上，追逐著我的小鹿；
追逐著美麗的野鹿兮，心兒相逐，
無論我走到哪裡，心都留在那蘇格蘭高地。

告別故鄉的高原兮，告別那北方，
她生就一顆勇敢的心，堅守價值；
我無論是遊蕩兮，還是流浪，
對故鄉山川的愛兮，永存心底。

告別那白雪覆蓋的高山峻嶺，
告別那寬闊的山谷和綠色的草坪；
告別那繁茂的森林和野生的灌木叢，
告別那湍急的河水和雷鳴般的山洪。

我的心留在那故鄉的高原兮，不在這裡，
我的心留在那高原上，追逐著我的小鹿；
追逐著美麗的野鹿兮，心兒相逐，
無論我走到哪裡，心都留在那蘇格蘭高地。

註：標題可譯為「我的心留在了高原」，但譯者以為「故鄉的高原」更好。

My Heart's in the Highlands

Robert Burns (1759 – 1796)

My heart's in the Highlands, my heart is not here,
My heart's in the Highlands, a-chasing the deer;
Chasing the wild-deer, and following the roe,
My heart's in the Highlands, wherever I go.

Farewell to the Highlands, farewell to the North,
The birth-place of Valour, the country of Worth ;
Wherever I wander, wherever I rove,
The hills of the Highlands for ever I love.

Farewell to the mountains, high-cover'd with snow,
Farewell to the straths and green vallies below;
Farewell to the forests and wild-hanging woods,
Farewell to the torrents and loud-pouring floods.

My heart's in the Highlands, my heart is not here,
My heart's in the Highlands, a-chasing the deer;
Chasing the wild-deer, and following the roe,
My heart's in the Highlands, wherever I go.

詩與愛

蘇軾　記夢見亡妻 [1]
十年生死不敢忘　陰陽兩界愛斷腸
卓文君　一二三　百千萬 [2]
數字愛情詩　萬千百　三二一
司馬相如羞愧面對賢惠妻

莎士比亞　對純潔青年以及青春的愛 [3]
用他永恆的詩行　讓青春隨著時間成長
狄金森　她對上帝的愛　化作夏天和音符 [4]
甚至　要讓自己的亡靈開出花朵
白朗寧夫人的至愛　至高至廣至深　至魂所及 [5]
是呼吸是微笑是眼淚　是整個生命
直到回歸上帝　愛的永恆　永不停息

從古到今　直至將來的永遠永遠
愛與人類共存　是人類生命的源泉
從南到北　從東到西　愛傳播到每一寸土地
詩表達愛情　有愛就會有詩　生命就有意義
愛讓文字熱情奔放　愛讓文字傾訴悲傷
愛讓文字情意綿綿　愛讓文字如膠似漆
詩言心　心中有愛　自然流淌的就是美麗的詩句
文字是詩的比丘之箭　射中的是有愛的心

註：
文中提到的詩均收集在本書中。
(1) 蘇軾 江城子・乙卯正月二十日夜記夢
(2) 卓文君的數字詩「細數我的情」
(3) 莎士比亞的十四行詩第 18 首「永恆的青春」
(4) 艾米莉·伊莉莎白·狄金森「永恆的生命」
(5) 白朗寧夫人的十四行詩「至愛」

Poetry and Love

SU Shi's dream of his deceased wife, after ten years of life [1]
And death apart, dare not forget, was a heartbroken mourning
ZHUO Wenjun's poem, from one two three, counted her deep love [2]
In numbers, up and then down, and her husband felt ashamed himself

Shakespeare's love of a fair youth [3]
Used his eternal lines to let the youth grow with time
Dickinson's love for God let herself be the summer [4]
And music notes, and wanted, even after death, her soul to bloom
Mrs Browning's love, to the highest, to the widest, to the deepest [5]
And to the soul's reach, was her breath, smile, and tears
Love is eternal and never ends

Forever and ever, the coexistence of love and human beings
Is the source of human life. From east to west
From south to north, love spreads to every inch of land
Poetry expresses love: where there is love, there will be poetry
And the life will be full of meanings
Love makes words passionate and unrestrained
Love makes words to express sorrow and sadness
Love makes words full of affection and emotion
Love makes words beautiful, sexy and attractive
Poetry speaks the heart: if there is love in the heart, the words
That flow naturally will form a beautiful poem
Words are the Cupid's arrows of a poem: whoever are hit
Are those with a heart of love

Footnote:
The poems quoted in this piece are all collected in this book.
1. SU Shi: Dream Recall
2. ZHUO Wenjun: Love of Countless
3. Shakespeare, Sonnet XVIII
4. Dickinson, Summer for thee, grant I may be
5. Browning, Sonnet XLIII

夕陽下的約定

打理自家花園中的園丁　　　　多想再次挽著你的手
悠閒的大腦裡思緒萬千：　　　在美麗的夕陽下散步
那年　那月　那天　　　　　　暢談當年湧動的青春
我們曾經有個夕陽下的約定　　橫幅　頭巾　口號　歌聲

當我們再回到那個廣場　　　　腦海裡浮現你的音容笑貌
不再會有那個惡魔的紀念堂　　還有你充滿陽光的自信
那雙手高擎火炬的女神　　　　那個時代的烙印
會讓我們淚眼婆娑　心潮蕩漾　無論過了多久也不會改變

你說過這是我們的責任　　　　多想對你說我們是最後的一代：
一定要看到自由的那一天　　　我們一定要中共法西斯倒台
可是劊子手的子彈　　　　　　我們一定要讓我們的下一代
結束了你年輕的生命　　　　　生活在一個自由的世界

Promise Under the Sunset

Doing some gardening work in the back garden
many thoughts come back in my leisurely brain:
On that day that month that year
we once made a promise under the sunset: —

When we returned to that square
there would be no memorial hall for that devil
The goddess with a torch in her hands
would make our eyes full of tears and our hearts bounce —

You told me it's our responsibility
to see that day of freedom arrives
but the CCP army's bullets
ended your young life of full of dreams!

Long for, once more, holding your hand
having a walk at the beautiful sunset
and chatting about the rallying youths
in that year: banners, bandanas, slogans and songs

Your voice and smiles appear before my eyes
and also your sunny self-confidence
the very imprint of that era, and this will be remembered
always, no matter how many years have passed

Long for telling you that we will be the last generation:
We must end the brutal Chinese Commufascism
We must succeed to let the next generations
to live in a world of free

紫色的夢

高貴的紫色
高貴的心靈會欣賞
思念　惆悵　遙望　遐想
如一絲一縷的長髮
萬般情感於一身
那年　那月　那日
曾經的曾經　我們是多麼的接近
那一顆紫色的太陽
那一個百年的夢想

Purple Dream

— To all dreamers of freedom

The noble purple
Will only be admired by a noble heart
Thinking of you, and longing for you
My thoughts are like strands of your beautiful long hair
You're looking into afar, full of calm emotions
On that day, that month, that year
Once before, we were so close and near
That noble purple Sun
That one hundred years of noble dream

狂想在中秋之夜

又是一個八月半兮 (1)
抬頭向青天把你尋覓
又大又圓的月亮兮
你那明亮清澈的眼睛
阿里山之風柔軟兮
日月潭水甜　可人兒更溫情
酸甜可口的蓮霧　多汁美味的鳳梨
自由台灣人自由的意志
遠隔重洋的你我兮　雖然從未見面
天上的月亮兮　代表了我的心 (2)

麗君的腳步兮
留在獅子山巔　香江水旁
點點漁火避風塘
鐘樓輕敲伴著麗人歌唱
自從來了窯洞的狸鼠兮
一切都改變了模樣
天堂的麗君兮　花好月圓之夜
地上的人兒思念兮　悲哀惆悵

君在前哨　麗君的聲音

輕喚人心兮　在水的那一邊

麗君用腳投票兮

從不踏上紅赤的土地

月未必是故土的圓兮

自由的人呼吸自由的空氣

思念是一張看不見的網兮

故鄉的親人與土地　在山的那一邊

十五的月亮一年又一年兮

惟盼月圓人圓不必太久

註：

(1) 農曆「八月半」是大陸有些地方中秋節之俗稱。

(2) 麗君，鄧麗君也。詩中借用了她唱過的歌曲中的一些詞語。參見：《月亮代表我的心》、《香港之夜》和《我的家在山的那一邊》。《君在前哨》是台灣人熟知的鄧麗君的勞軍演唱系列。

Rhapsody of the Night of Mid-Autumn

Again at the night of Mid-Autumn [1]
Look up into the starlit sky to find you:
the full moon, big and bright, like your bright and clear eyes.
The wind of Mt Alishan is soft, and the water [2]
in the Sun Moon Lake sweet, but people even tender
Sweet and sour wax jambu, and juicy pineapples, both delicious
represent the free will of the free Taiwanese
You and I, separated by oceans, have never met
but the clear moon resembles my heart

Teresa's footsteps printed on the top [3]
of the Lion Mountain and the Xiangjiang riverside
Dotted fishing lights at typhoon shelter bays
and the soft echoing bell tower once accompanied the beauty to sing.
Ever since the raccoon came out of the cave
everything has changed beyond recognition
Teresa's now in the heaven, as if a lotus on the moon
She's dearly missed by Hong Kong

Teresa's at the Outpost, and her voice
and whispering are echoed across the strait
Teresa voted with her feet
and never set her feet on the reddened land.
The moon may not be the fullest over the home town
and free people must breathe the air of free
The longing's an invisible web: The relatives
and my birthplace are on the other side of the mountain.
The Mid-Autumn moon do come year after year
I wish that the next full moon
and people's free reunion wouldn't be too long

Footnote:
1. The Mid-Autumn Festival is on the 15th day of August in the lunar calendar.
2. Mt Alishan and Sun Moon Lake are beautiful sightseeing places in Taiwan.
3. Teresa Teng, the late Taiwanese singer who lived in Hong Kong for many years. Some phrases in the second and third stanzas have been borrowed from some of her songs, like The Moon Represents My Heart, Hong Kong at Night and My Home Is Over the Mountain. Teresa's at the Outpost is a series of TV programs in which Miss Teng entertained the Taiwanese troops on the frontier.

夢中的故鄉、夢中的河

我童年的村莊四面都有河
一年四季繞著村子不停地流
東面一座三條石板的小石橋
西面一條彎曲細長的河上土堤壩路
村子古代的模樣在我的腦海裏描呀描
假如東西二邊都曾經有一座吊橋
那我的村子就是一座天然的城堡

石橋下常年有清澈的河水
自由自在的魚兒在橋下游
這就是我記憶裏的童年歲月
雨中的土堤壩呀滿是泥巴
冬天的土堤壩呀格外的滑
不管風吹雨打、不管嚴寒酷夏
土堤壩路總是看著我上學、回家

「農業學大寨」野蠻地向河流要田
村西的土堤壩被挖、村東的小河被填平
「鬥天鬥地」徹底毀壞了村子的風水
若干年以後，以「城市化」的名義
我美麗的村子噢！被夷為平地！
曾經的村莊喲只能存留於記憶
曾經的河流喲只能流淌在夢裏

中國人百年的夢是生活在自由之地
中國社會的現狀依然令人不勝唏噓！

The Home Town in My Dreams,
So Is the River

The village of my birthplace was surrounded
by rivers which were flowing all year round
A small stone bridge with three long slabs on its east side
and curved and narrow river with a levee on the west side
The ancient appearance of the village was depicted in my mind:
If there used to be a suspension bridge on both the sides of east and west
then my village would had been a natural castle, or could!

The water was clear in the river, and fish
could be seen to swim freely under the bridge
This has been kept in my childhood memories —
The road on the levee in the rain was muddy
which in winter was extremely slippery
No matter if it's windy or rainy
a bitter winter or scorching summer day
the levee road always watched me, each weekday
going to school and returning home

"Learn from Dazhai in agriculture": The east river was converted
into farming fields, and the levee on the west side was dug up
as well for rivers had to be straightened, mad
"Fight against heaven and earth" completely destroyed
the natural beauty of the village of childhood!
A few decades later, in the name of "urbanization", o alas!
my beautiful village! was razed to the ground!
The village now can only exist in my memory
and the rivers can only flow in my dreams!

The century-old dream of the Chinese has been to live in a land of free
but the CCP's China is a world shame, and unease!

Footnote:
- "Learn from Dazhai in agriculture" was the CCP's campaign in 1960s, in which every inch of ground, including mountains and rivers and lakes, must be converted into farming fields for growing crops, and, as a result, the huge damage had been done to the nature.
- "Fight against heaven and earth": The CCP doesn't believe in God, and doesn't allow any other religions but communism.

愛爾蘭民歌：來吧，我心上的人

作者：不詳

希望我在那個遠處的山上
坐在那裡哭到天老地荒
直到每一滴淚都能讓水輪啓動磨坊
親愛的，願你平安無恙

來吧，來吧，我心上的人
優雅從容，如履輕雲
就在那扇邊門，我們一起私奔
親愛的，願你一帆風順

賣掉採來的石塊，賣掉紡好的捲軸線
賣掉唯一的紡車，它一直跟在我的身邊
買一把鋒利的鋼劍送給我所愛的人
親愛的，願你無往而不勝

給我的襯裙染色，鮮紅燦爛
即使我滿世界為了糊口而討飯
直到我的父母不希望再見到我回來
親愛的，願你不要猶豫徘徊

希望我心上的人從法國回來
想必他在那裡名利雙收，八方風采
假如我們再次相會，將是命運的安排
親愛的，願你平平安安歸來

註：

這首傳統的愛爾蘭民歌 "Siúil a Rún" 有好幾個版本。根據維基，它的歷史不詳，或許與英國十七世紀的「光榮革命（Glorious Revolution）」之間的「飛雁（Flight of the Wild Geese）」有關。在愛爾蘭歷史上，「雁（Wild Geese）」是指在十六至十八世紀去歐洲大陸服役的愛爾蘭士兵。由於該歌有好幾個版本，本文是其中之一（*），作者不詳，這一版本似乎更有鄉土氣息。

（*）https://celtic-lyrics.com/lyrics/458.html

Siúil a Rún

Unknown

I wish I was on yonder hill
Tis there I'd sit and cry my fill
Till every tear would turn a mill
Is go dte tu mo mhuirnin slan

Siuil, siuil, siuil a ruin
Siuil go sochair agus siuil go ciuin
Siuil go doras agus ealaigh liom
Is go dte tu mo mhuirnin slan

I'll sell my rock, I'll sell my reel
I'll sell my only spinning wheel
to buy my love a sword of steel
Is go dte tu mo mhuirnin slan

I'll dye my petticoats, I'll dye them red
and it's round the World I will beg for bread
until my parents would wish me dead
Is go dte tu mo mhuirnin slan

I wish my love would return from France
his fame and fortune there advanced
If we meet again, 't will be by chance
Is go dte tu mo mhuirnin slan

Footnote:
The literal English meaning of the second stanza is as follows.
Walk, walk, walk my love
Walk gracefully and walk quietly
Walk to a door and run away with me
I wish you well
See https://celtic-lyrics.com/lyrics/458.html

綠島之歌

這綠島
不沉的航母
她的歌聲
是智者先賢幾千年的暢想
呵　綠島小夜曲 (1)
心的渴望　愛的絕唱

喜瑪拉雅為你祝福
溫柔的淚珠化作雲祥
祈禱你的幸福安寧
泰山終日翹首
盼著從綠島升起的朝陽

呵　綠島之夜　迷人 (2)
令人鍾情的灣灣姑娘
不管你白人黑人黃種人
不管你基督徒佛教徒法輪大法修煉者
灣灣姑娘張開雙手擁抱
個人自由　傳統倫理　宗教文化
普世價值　東方西方　其樂融融
譜寫世界文明之和諧交響

一百多年前北伐的硝煙
瀰漫依然　紅色陰霾
伴隨黃土高原的塵埃
北風刺虐　欲蓋彌彰

貧瘠的土地　乾裂　缺氧
枯萎的玫瑰　眷念甘甜的雨露
藍色的天空　自由的陽光

東方之珠　悲哀的香江
啊　黃河　忘記了咆哮
遠古的歌謠　忘記了曲調
啊　長江　忘記了歡唱
幸福的源泉　忘記了慈祥
澳澳　香香　回歸鳥籠
在山的那一邊　惆悵 (3)
紅樓之夢依然在紅樓
老佛爺的小腳　依然日夜奔忙

這綠島
面對黃土高坡　在水一方
演奏著太平洋動人的旋律
華夏的夢想
灣灣　我愛你呵
為自由而驕傲的姑娘

註：

(1) 《綠島小夜曲》來龍去脈，參見 https://blog.xuite.net/wild.fun/blog/33954011

(2) 《綠島之夜》https://song.corp.com.tw/mv.aspx?id=50325

(3) 《家在山那邊》https://zh.wikipedia.org/zh-tw/ 家在山那邊

Song of a Green Island

This green island
is an unsinkable carrier of aircraft
Her singing of freedom is the dream
of sages for thousands of years
O! *Serenade of Green Island*
the song of love, the desire of lover's heart

Blessed by Himalayas
with its clouds full of joyful tears
for your peace and happiness
Mt Tai looks up all day long to hear your song
and eagerly waits, from the green island
for the rising bright sun

O! *Night at the Green Island* is charming
as a sunny and sexy girl of Taiwanese angel
No matter if you're black, white or brown
a Christian, Buddhism or Falun Dafa practitioner
you're welcomed with open arms by the angel
Here the harmonious symphony of world civilizations
is composed by individual freedom, traditional ethics
culture of different religions, universal values
of the East and West

Across the Taiwan Strait
the smoke of the Northern Expedition
a hundred more years ago
is still spreading, mixed with the red haze
accompanied by the dust of Loess Plateau
The northerly wind stabs and bares its fangs
while masked with a smile face
The barren land's dry, of hypoxia, and cracked
and the withered roses long for the sweet dew
blue sky, green land and sunlight of free

O alas! the Yellow River long forgot to roar —
ancient ballads with forgotten tunes
O alas! the Yangtze also forgot to sing —
the source of happiness with forgotten kindness
Macau and Hong Kong are now the birds in a cage!
Teresa Teng's melancholy *On the Other Side of Mountain*
still is echoing across the mountain
The Dream of the Red Mansions
still is dreaming in the forbidden red mansions
The little feet of Empress Dowager Cixi
still are walking, hurriedly and harshly, night and day

This green green island
Facing the Loess Plateau across the water
is conducting the melody of the Pacific Ocean
the dream of all the Chinese today
The angel of Taiwan I love you
as you're the proudest girl of liberty

淚水，莫名的淚水

英國 阿爾弗雷德，丁尼生勳爵 (1809–1892)

淚水，莫名的淚水，莫名其詳，
它源於具有某種神聖性的深層的失望
從心底升起，至眼泉中湧出。
看著喜人的田野秋色，回想
一去不復返的往日時光。

如同照亮船帆的第一束晨光，
將我們的朋友從冥界送回一樣令人興奮，也象
映紅船帆的最後一片晚霞將我們所愛的人
沉沒在邊際線下一樣令人悲傷；
如此悲傷，又如此興奮，流逝的往日時光。

啊，悲傷又奇異，就象在黑暗的夏日
黎明 半醒的晨鳥為臨終的人歌唱，
慢慢升起的朝陽將方型的窗戶
投影在垂死的眼睛之上；
如此悲傷，又如此奇異，流逝的往日時光。

如同記憶裡與故人的親吻一樣稀珍，
也象那些無果的慾望一樣甜蜜 想像中的唇吻
被他人享有；如同情愛一樣的熱烈，
如同初戀，狂野而滿懷遺憾；
哦，人生中的死亡，流逝的往日時光！

註：這是丁尼生勳爵所著《公主（The Princess）》中的一首歌。根據《每天一首詩》(*)，
他曾經描述，這首歌的創作靈感來自廷特恩修道院（Tintern Abbey）的金黃色秋景，
充滿了他過去的記憶，往日的激情。

(*) Albery, Nicholas. Poem for the Day, The Natural Death Centre, 1997.

Tears, Idle Tears

Alfred, Lord Tennyson (1809-1892)

Tears, idle tears, I know not what they mean,
Tears from the depth of some divine despair
Rise in the heart, and gather to the eyes,
In looking on the happy autumn-fields,
And thinking of the days that are no more.

Fresh as the first beam glittering on a sail,
That brings our friends up from the underworld,
Sad as the last which reddens over one
That sinks with all we love below the verge;
So sad, so fresh, the days that are no more.

Ah, sad and strange as in dark summer dawns
The earliest pipe of half-awakened birds
To dying ears, when unto dying eyes
The casement slowly grows a glimmering square;
So sad, so strange, the days that are no more.

Dear as remembered kisses after death,
And sweet as those by hopeless fancy feigned
On lips that are for others; deep as love,
Deep as first love, and wild with all regret;
O Death in Life, the days that are no more!

致向日葵

日本 野口米次郎 (1875–1947)

你的真性情突然釋放：
墨守成規的我們是多麼悲傷！
你生命中燃燒的每一個原子都是奇蹟，
你活得多麼充實！
難道你從未想過要轉向冷酷和陰暗？
熱情陽光的肝膽，
是青春和驕傲的標誌；
你是一首絢麗多彩的抒情詩；
你無聲的歌聲是行動和志氣。
你生命的意義多麼令人著迷。
驚嘆於你的清醒意識，—
你的生活方式具有偉大的意義！

註：向日葵是烏克蘭的國花。2022 年 2 月 24 日，俄國發動了對烏克蘭的侵略戰爭。
歷史會記住這一天。

To The Sunflower

Yone Noguchi (1875-1947)

Thou burstest from mood:
How sad we have to cling to experience!
Marvel of thy every atom burning of life,
How fully thou livest!
Didst thou ever think to turn to cold and shadow?
Passionate liver of sunlight,
Symbol of youth and pride;
Thou art a lyric of thy soaring colour;
Thy voicelessness of song is action.
What absorption of thy life's meaning.
Wonder of thy consciousness,—
Mighty sense of thy existence!

當你老了的時候

愛爾蘭 威廉·巴特勒·耶次 (1865-1939)

當你老了的時候，白髮滿頭，濃濃睡意，
坐在壁爐旁打盹，取下書架上的這本書，
慢慢地閱讀，回憶你曾經的樣子
深色的眼影，眼睛酷似那溫柔的瀑布；

想一想曾經有多少人喜歡你的優雅與陽光，
他們愛你的美麗，是假意還是真情，
可有一個人，他愛著你躁動不安的魂靈，
也愛那歲月變化在你臉上留下來的憂傷；

想像中，你彎下腰照看爐火時的喃喃自語
有些悲傷和失望，愛你的人已經離開
白天　他在高高的山岡上踱步、徘徊
夜晚　他在天上，隱藏在一群閃爍的星星裡。

When You Are Old

William Butler Yeats (1865-1939)

When you are old and grey and full of sleep,
And nodding by the fire, take down this book,
And slowly read, and dream of the soft look
Your eyes had once, and of their shadows deep;

How many loved your moments of glad grace,
And loved your beauty with love false or true,
But one man loved the pilgrim soul in you,
And loved the sorrows of your changing face;

And bending down beside the glowing bars,
Murmur, a little sadly, how Love fled
And paced upon the mountains overhead
And hid his face amid a crowd of stars.

很想你在這裡

我獨自一人
想你 想你想得很疼

記得你說
不要想入非非
我無法控制
這不安分的思緒

我獨自一人
想你 想你想得很疼

感覺無助
可你不屑一顧
我無法控制
這般想你的思緒

很想 很想你在這裡
此時我獨自一人

我獨自一人
想你 想你想得很疼

我獨自一人
想你想你想得很疼

Wish You Were Here

When I'm alone
my feeling's strong

Heard you say
don't carry away
But I can't help it
'cause my sleepless mind

When I'm alone
my feeling is strong

I'm despair
as you don't care
But I can't help it
'cause my longing mind

Wish you were here
when I'm alone

When I'm alone
my feeling's strong

When I'm alone
my feeling's strong

生活與生命
Life

生命的寬度　而不是長度
　　才是對生命的測量
生命的價值　不在於呼吸了多少口氣
　　而在於有幾口是蕩氣迴腸

It's the breadth of life, not the length
　　That measures the meaning of life
The value of a life isn't counted by
　　How many breaths taken but that taken away

永恆的生命

美國 艾米莉·伊莉莎白·狄金森（1830－1886）

啊　讓我是你的夏天
當夏季已經過去！
我也是你的音樂　當夜鷹
和黃鸝 — 沒了聲音！

我的魂靈將離開墓地　為你綻放
奉獻我的花朵！
請你來採摘我 —
銀蓮花兒 —
這是你的花 — 地久天長！

註：標題「永恆的生命」為譯者所加。

Summer for thee, grant I may be

Emily Elizabeth Dickinson (1830 – 1886)

Summer for thee, grant I may be
When Summer days are flown!
Thy music still, when Whippoorwill
And Oriole — are done!

For thee to bloom, I'll skip the tomb
And row my blossoms o'er!
Pray gather me —
Anemone —
Thy flower — forevermore!

荷包牡丹

美國 麗莎·庫珀

在大自然的子宮裡　躁動不安
紅色的花朵　鮮豔　斑斕
嫻靜的枝芽　似燃燒的火焰
靈感裡溢出美麗的詩篇

綠葉綠色構成油畫的背景
紅花魚貫成行　匆忙的場面
大地母親堅強的意志
播下易於繁殖的種子

生命的動力　春天的大潮
誘導芬芳淳樸的幼苗
在避風的地方　快快成長
與姐妹們一起競相開放

精心展示的一顆顆心
看似在滴血　躬身笑對秋天
享受大自然的庇佑　縱然是沉睡
也在策劃來年的爭奇鬥艷

註：Lamprocapnos spectabilis，中文名：荷包牡丹、瓔珞牡丹等。
英文名：bleeding heart（滴血的心）。

Bleeding Hearts

Lisa Cooper

Restless in nature's womb
Vivid tis fuchsine bloom
Lulling shoots afire
Beauteous prose inspire

Canvas panoramic green
Abreast tempest scene
Gaia's steadfast creed
Plotted tis fruitful seed

Breath life springtide
Balmy callow guide
Urge seedlings alee
Bestow thine pedigree

Bleeding heart adorn
Bow to autumn scorn
Sheltered in nature's keep
Conspire whilst fast asleep

生命的寬度

一
上帝是公平的
每一個生命　只有一次
也只有一次機會
生命得以展示

生命的長度是有限的
然而　上帝仁慈
讓每一個生命
可以擁有無限的寬度

二
有些遺臭萬年的生命
給人類造成了深重的災難
對惡魂的崇拜
生命本身變得可恥

在人類的精神世界裡
是那些點燃著人類智慧的生命
賦予生命以意義
這樣的生命　寬度無限

三
生命不可能扔了再來
每一個生命是同等的寶貴
對別的生命的蔑視
就是對自身的作賤

每個生命具有同等的權利
尊重這種權利是對自身的尊重
有些生命之所以遺臭萬年
是因為它們剝奪了這種權利

四
生命的寬度　而不是長度
才是對生命的測量
生命的價值　不在於呼吸了多少口氣
而在於有幾口是蕩氣迴腸

不少寬廣的生命是短暫的
但正是這些優秀的生命
賦予了人類真正的靈魂
照亮著人類前行的道路

五
患了「阿 Q 綜合症」的生命是可悲的
更可悲的是不知道自己是患者
這樣的生命越多　越長
社會的災難越深重

自娛自樂的生命可以是幸福快樂的
然而 能帶給人類幸福快樂的
是那些慈悲的生命　是那些思考的生命
是那些先天下之憂而憂的生命

Breadth Of Life

(1)
God is fair
Each life has only one lifetime
And has only one chance
For it to reveal

Life has a limited length
Yet the merciful God
Let each life
Can have an unlimited breadth

(2)
Some notorious lives
Cause great sufferings to human beings
Worshipping these evil spirits
Makes one's own life shameful

In the spiritual world
Only those lives that ignite human wisdom
Make life meaningful
The breadth of such life is limitless

(3)
One's life can't be recycled
And all lives are equal and precious
Disregarding other lives
Actually is a self disrespect

All lives have equal rights
Respecting this right is a self respect
Some lives are infamous in history
For they deprived other's human rights

(4)

It's the breadth of life, not the length
That measures the meaning of life
The value of a life isn't counted by
How many breaths taken but that taken away

Many broad lives are short
Yet it's these great lives
That are the real soul of all humanity
And light up the way for future

(5)

It's sad to see the Stockholm syndrome suffers
Yet the saddest to see some unaware of their illness
The more such lives, and the longer they have this disease
The more the whole society will suffer

Self entertaining lives can be joyful
But that can really bring mankind happiness
Are those compassionate and thoughtful lives, and those
Who worry about the humanity before themselves

共處共存

澳大利亞 羅伯特·莫瑞·史密斯

何時學會欣賞
那些我們眼前的
生命的美麗？

蜻蜓
直升機般地飛來飛去
展示它的舞姿

鳥兒
每天日常的工作
讓你我看見

抬頭觀望今天的天空吧
或許會見到穿梭的
小小藍鶯

甚至小棕鼠
也有
忙碌的一天

一切生命
過著自己的日子
相處共存

Coexistence

Robert Murray Smith

When will you know
the beauty
of life, in
full sight?

The beauty of
a dragonfly,
helicopter like,
darting to and fro
for all to see.

The birds in daily
tasks, to be seen
by you, and me.

Look for a tiny
blue wren rushing
through the sky
today.

Even a little brown
rat scurrying through
its day.

For all creatures live
in life, to coexist.

Robert Murray Smith *(c), 2017*
Adelaide, Australia
My copyright is asserted.

奇遇

三瓣絲瓜花，真的很奇葩！
通常是五瓣，偶爾也見四瓣、六瓣花。
是基因變異，還是大自然的魔力？
無論如何，這是上天給我的驚喜。

某年、某月、某天，
你生命中的邂逅一定會出現。
他／她的出現，給你驚喜。
愛，是人生中最偉大的奇遇。

Encounter

A three-petal loofah flower is really joyous
Usually five petals, occasionally four or six.
Is it the result of genetic mutation, by chance
Or a new course that the nature changes?
Nonetheless, this really is a given surprise!

On a certain day, a certain month, a certain year,
An encounter in your life is bound to transpire.
The come by of him or her will surprise you.
Love is the life's greatest adventure.

永恆的青春

英國 威廉·莎士比亞 (1564 – 1616)

譯者的話:在查詢「Darling Buds of May」時發現,該詞出自莎士比亞的十四行詩 XVIII。讀完之後,我彷彿看到了一九八九年天安門廣場上湧動著的青春熱血。故嘗試翻譯,並以此獻給勇敢的青年們。

青春可以比作夏天吧

可她的美更加溫柔　動人　看啊 —

粗野的風　總想吹落五月迷人的花蕾 (1)

夏天的好日子太短了 —

偶爾　太陽當空時太熱了

時常　烏雲遮蓋了金色的陽光

一切美好的東西都會衰退 —

是隨機的　還是大自然的魔力

然而　不朽的是青春呵 —

她擁有的美麗不會消失

死亡也奈何不了她

這永恆的詩行　讓青春隨著時間成長

　　只要人能夠呼吸　眼睛能夠看見

　　只要生命不息　青春就有活力

註:標題「永恆的青春」為譯者所加。

(1) 在莎士比亞時代,五月已是夏季。

Sonnet XVIII

William Shakespeare (1564 – 1616)

Shall I compare thee to a summer's day?
Thou art more lovely and more temperate:
Rough winds do shake the darling buds of May,
And summer's lease hath all too short a date:
Sometime too hot the eye of heaven shines,
And often is his gold complexion dimmed,
And every fair from fair sometime declines,
By chance, or nature's changing course untrimmed:
But thy eternal summer shall not fade,
Nor lose possession of that fair thou ow'st,
Nor shall death brag thou wander'st in his shade,
When in eternal lines to time thou grow'st,
      So long as men can breathe, or eyes can see,
      So long lives this, and this gives life to thee.

屬靈的激動與歡樂

美國 吉木·F·瓦格利

我現在明白兮：我應該做風箏的尾飄！
以多種不同的方式，在天空翔翱！
在這些人生的高潮中兮；抵達多重之高！
把現實世界短暫地忘記兮；看起來真的重要。

坐在可控速的兩個輪子上兮：我要上揚！
飛行在水面上方，我的風箏會自行膨脹！
帶著榮耀，思考我有福的日子兮，
每一次的升高，都會激動萬分、心情歡暢！

我的靈魂之旅兮：我珍惜！
然而不幸的是；我已經體力不支。
現在這些精神之體驗兮，
通過閱讀經文，領會聖靈的教誨來實行！

帆傘和摩托車兮，曾帶給我歡樂的時光！
可是屬靈的，玩具不會再有用場。

Euphoria

Jim F Wagley

I see now! I'm going to be the tail of the kite!
In many different ways, I would begin to take flight!
In these life highs; reaching many levels of height!
To leave the world behind briefly; only seemed right.

On two wheels with speed; I would begin to levitate!
When soaring over water; my kite would inflate!
As I pondered my sacred day with glory of,
Each flying case; reaching levels in euphoria!

My spiritual experiences; I cherished!
Then sadly; my physical ability perished.
Now those Spiritual experiences are wrought,
By reading scriptures, of what the Holy Ghost has taught!

The parasail and motorcycle brought days of joy!
But the Spiritual; no longer achieved by a toy.

Jim F Wagley, USA
Copyright 2019, All Rights Reserved

自由的孩子

題記：為了自由的孩子，更為了孩子的自由

哦　親愛的寶貝快快長大
媽媽要告訴你一句話
「你媽媽的言論被監控過」
這曾經發生在我們民主的國家

哦　親愛的寶貝不用害怕
我們生活在民有民治民享的國家
人權和言論自由是普世價值
誰也不可違背美國的憲法

註：受愷萊·麥克恩萊在 2020 年 10 月 15 日所發推文的啟發，她的推文說：「有一天，我會告訴她什麼是（言論）審查，而且為了發聲，她不得不昧著良心刪除媽媽的推文！」。麥克恩萊曾是川普政府時期的第 31 屆白宮新聞秘書。

106

Free Child

— To all freedom loving mothers

O please grow up fast my sweetheart
I want to tell you Mommy's tweet
was once grossly censored
on our free democratic land

O my darling baby don't be fearful
as our country is of, by, and for the people
Human rights and free speech are universal values
that the US constitution guarantees

Footnote:
This poem is inspired by Kayleigh McEnany's tweet on 15 October 2020 — "One day I will explain to her what censorship is and why she had to unjustly delete Mommy's tweet in order to speak!"

客西馬尼果園 1914-18

英國 魯德亞德·吉卜林 (1865-1936)

一個名為客西馬尼的果園兮，
曾經坐落在法國北部的皮卡第，
人們到了那裡
目睹英國的士兵們一個一個地死去。
我們曾經走過 — 我們曾經走過兮
或者停息，也許，
運送防護面具以防止毒氣
擴散到客西馬尼園子外的區域。

就在那個客西馬尼果園兮，
有一位美麗的少女，
當她和我説話之時
我卻不停地祈禱我能夠避免戰爭的悲劇。
我的長官坐在椅子上兮，
戰友們躺在綠草地，
當我們在那兒停息之時
我不停地祈禱我能夠避免戰爭的悲劇。

沒有幸免 — 沒有幸免兮
我沒有能夠逃脫戰爭的悲劇。
我喝下了命運的苦酒兮
當我們在客西馬尼園子外吸入了毒氣！

註：客西馬尼果園在耶路撒冷，根據《新約聖經》，耶穌被釘死在十字架上的前
夜，與他的門徒們在最後的晚餐之後前往此處禱告。這裡，詩人借用了聖經裡面
的故事。對英文詩的解讀，正如有關文獻指出的，正確理解詩中的 pass 和 cup 兩
個詞是最關鍵的。

Gethsemane 1914-18

Rudyard Kipling (1865-1936)

The Garden called Gethsemane
In Picardy it was,
And there the people came to see
The English soldiers pass.
We used to pass — we used to pass
Or halt, as it might be,
And ship our masks in case of gas
Beyond Gethsemane.

The Garden called Gethsemane,
It held a pretty lass,
But all the time she talked to me
I prayed my cup might pass.
The officer sat on the chair,
The men lay on the grass,
And all the time we halted there
I prayed my cup might pass.

It didn't pass — it didn't pass
It didn't pass from me.
I drank it when we met the gas
Beyond Gethsemane!

春誕的種子

英國 愷韻·維特尼

內儲的光能
在棲息的殼子裡
翻騰、已甦醒。

心底的欲念
在舊生命中蠕動
要重新呈現。

生命的渴求
重組過去的形態
將萌生新苗。

原作者註：
春誕 (Imbolc) 在 2 月 1 日左右，慶祝日照時間的漸漸變長，並為新年作好準備。

譯者註：
春誕：春天的誕生，類似立春的第一天。亦稱為聖布里吉德節
（St Brigid's Day）或聖燭節（Candlemas）。

Imbolc's Seed

Kaaren Whitney

Potent light within
protected by habit's shell
stirs, rouses itself.

Intention forms
rustles inside old choices
seeks fresh expression

echoes life's longing
restructuring past patterns
new growth will come soon.

最後的十四行詩

英國 約翰·濟慈 (1795 – 1821)

耀眼之星 [1]，若我與你一樣亙久不變 —
不是閃亮而孤獨地高掛在夜空，
一直瞪著大大的眼睛，
像大自然耐心而不眠的虔誠的隱士，
看著湧動的潮水，像神父般地
給地球人類的海岸以聖潔的洗禮，
或者注視著輕輕飄落的雪花
覆蓋群山與荒原 —
不是 — 而是依舊亙久、依舊不變，
頭枕在美麗愛人成熟的乳房，
永遠感受它輕柔的起伏跌蕩，
在甜蜜的不安分之中我永遠無眠，
　　依舊、依舊聽著她那溫馨的呼吸，
　　永遠這樣地活著 — 否則不如歸去。

註：
(1)「耀眼之星」有分析是指北極星。

112

Last Sonnet

John Keats (1795 – 1821)

Bright star, would I were steadfast as thou art –
Not in lone splendour hung aloft the night,
And watching, with eternal lids apart,
Like Nature's patient sleepless Eremite,
The moving waters at their priest-like task
Of pure ablution round earth's human shores,
Or gazing on the new soft-fallen mask
Of snow upon the mountains and the moors –
No-yet still steadfast, still unchangeable,
Pillowed upon my fair love's ripening breast,
To feel for ever its soft fall and swell,
Awake for ever in a sweet unrest,
    Still, still to hear her tender-taken breath,
    And so live ever – or else swoon to death.

生命的軌跡

英國 萊蒂蒂婭·伊麗莎白·蘭敦 (1802–1838)

─────────

作為早年孤獨的孩子，我早就學會
讓我的內心自我滿足，而且自我尋求
在心靈深處的同情和支持。

─────────

好吧，看懂我的表情，凝視我的眼睛，─
　　它們經過了過分嚴格的教育和訓練
我靈魂深處的一個秘密即將道破，
　　一個隱藏的想法就要暴露。

從不知道是什麼時候的事情
　　我可以隨意地探視我的內心；
它曾被恐嚇與膽怯壓抑，
　　現在則是被告誡教訓。

我生活在冷酷、虛假的群體，
　　而我必須看上去與他人沒有差異；
我這個樣子，因我的虛偽
　　讓我變成我最討厭的其中之一。

我調教我的嘴唇，讓它露出最甜美的微笑，
　　我的舌頭吐出最溫柔的音調；
假別人相似的行為，直到
　　幾乎將我自己的個性丟掉。

我經受那些阿附上層的冠冕堂皇的檢視，
　　無論我要說什麼東西；
在社交活動中，所有人像盲人一樣，
　　不得不學會感覺他們生活的排場。

我核查自己的想法，就像
　　被鞍轡之馬與韁繩的博弈；
我讓我的情感，像沉船一樣
　　躺在深不可測的海底。

我聽他們八卦性愛、隱私。
　　真人實事，取笑別人的名字；
嘲笑一切神聖與創世的真理，
　　而我也是如此。

我聽他們講述一些感人的離奇故事，
　　我嚥下眼淚；
我聽他們例舉一些慷慨的行為，
　　而我學會了譏笑諷刺。

我聽到有關心靈、善良、純潔，
　　然而只是在歡樂玩笑中談及；
直到所有的德性，噫！甚至希望，
　　似乎從地球上流亡。

有一種恐懼，尖刻的譏誚挖苦，
　　是我之所以憂慮的全部。
一根馬鬃懸掛著的利劍
　　永遠在頭的上面。

我們向極其奴性的信仰鞠躬，
　　活在最低三下四的恐懼之中；
可是我們中間沒有人敢講
　　那些沒有人會選擇聽到的真相。

即使我們夢有崇高的理想，
　　軟弱就會讓它泡湯；
而且，懶惰與浮華時尚
　　是我們自己把桎梏戴上。

毫無疑問，我絕不是為此而生！
　　我感覺有一種更高尚的信念
具有慈善的力量，堅定的意志，
　　不經意間讓我不會獨寂！

我仰望，繁星閃亮
　　裝點午夜的天穹；
我希望，非常熱切地希望，
　　像星星一樣發光。

我有如此強烈的渴望
　造福人類；
彷彿有一種不朽的力量
　主宰我的思想。

我想著那盞長明燈，
　點亮了塵世間的陰霾。
它讓死亡的榮耀，
　墳墓的未來 ─

即塵世的未來，更像是來自
　天間標誌性的暗示；
─ 一個邁步、單詞、聲音、眼神，─
　唉呀！我的夢已經完成！

還有這個世界，以及令人丟臉的骯髒，
　也在我的靈魂裡隱藏；
身處這個毫無價值的群體
　我僅僅是其中的一個無名分子。

為何描寫這個我？因為我的內心
　嚮往著未來的春天，
那個未來熱愛翔翔
　勝過乘上雄鷹的翅膀。

我們的現在，屬於永恆的時空
　但僅是一個斑點，我在其中
為失去的希望找到歸宿，
　那是我的靈魂所熟悉的月宮。

哦！我不是我自己，— 我是什麼？—
　　沒有任何價值而且怯懦，
我的每一個私自的念頭，都像
　　一抹羞怯的紅暈熾灼面龐。

但詩歌似火焰燃著我的嘴唇。
　　讓我的心成為聖地；
因為它本身神聖，
　　儘管被熔塑，被貶低。

我是我自己，在生命的束縛之鏈上
　　我僅僅是卑鄙的一環；
可我也作過受尊崇的演講，
　　哦，不必再空談！

我的第一個、最後一個、唯一的願望，
　　是想知道我迷人的詩行
會不會在榮耀的晨光中甦醒，
　　再一次重溫我的諾言？

那位年輕的少女，當她的眼淚
　　獨自在月光下閃亮 —
她的淚為離去的和所愛的人流淌 —
　　會不會輕聲將我的詩歌吟唱？

在昏暗的油燈旁邊，那位白皙的青年，
　　他自己的火焰奄奄一息，
會不會從身邊的諸多卷軸古籍，
　　看上那一卷刻有我的名字？

　對於沉默的已故之人
　　評價不要那麼不值一文；
我並不在乎，在生命消逝之後
　　我的靈魂是否長存。

註：蘭敦女士是英國維多利亞時代的一位富有才華而又多產的詩人與作家，她名字的縮寫 L. E. L. 更為人所知，可惜在 36 歲時不幸去世。這一首長詩是作者的內心獨白。在今天看來，對社會的大一統與人的自由個性、文學藝術作品的永恆價值、以及生命的意義等等的看法依然鮮活。值得一提的是，有人指出，這首詩的標題可能是暗指或者是回應莎士比亞的第 16 首十四行詩，參見
https://phdessay.com/reading-response-lines-of-life-landon/。

Lines of Life

Letitia Elizabeth Landon (1802 – 1838)

———————

Orphan in my first years, I early learnt
To make my heart suffice itself, and seek
Support and sympathy in its own depths.

———————

Well, read my cheek, and watch my eye, —
　　Too strictly school'd are they
One secret of my soul to show,
　　One hidden thought betray.

I never knew the time my heart
　　Look'd freely from my brow;
It once was check'd by timidness,
　　'Tis taught by caution now.

I live among the cold, the false,
　　And I must seem like them;
And such I am, for I am false
　　As those I most condemn.

I teach my lip its sweetest smile,
　　My tongue its softest tone;
I borrow others' likeness, till
　　Almost I lose my own.

I pass through flattery's gilded sieve,
　　Whatever I would say;
In social life, all, like the blind,
　　Must learn to feel their way.

I check my thoughts like curbed steeds
    That struggle with the rein;
I bid my feelings sleep, like wrecks
    In the unfathom'd main.

I hear them speak of love, the deep.
    The true, and mock the name;
Mock at all high and early truth,
    And I too do the same.

I hear them tell some touching tale,
    I swallow down the tear;
I hear them name some generous deed,
    And I have learnt to sneer.

I hear the spiritual, the kind,
    The pure, but named in mirth;
Till all of good, ay, even hope,
    Seems exiled from our earth.

And one fear, withering ridicule,
    Is all that I can dread;
A sword hung by a single hair
    For ever o'er the head.

We bow to a most servile faith,
    In a most servile fear;
While none among us dares to say
    What none will choose to hear.

And if we dream of loftier thoughts,
    In weakness they are gone;
And indolence and vanity
    Rivet our fetters on.

Surely I was not born for this!
    I feel a loftier mood
Of generous impulse, high resolve,
    Steal o'er my solitude!

I gaze upon the thousand stars
    That fill the midnight sky;
And wish, so passionately wish,
    A light like theirs on high.

I have such eagerness of hope
    To benefit my kind;
And feel as if immortal power
    Were given to my mind.

I think on that eternal fame,
    The sun of earthly gloom.
Which makes the gloriousness of death,
    The future of the tomb —

That earthly future, the faint sign
    Of a more heavenly one;
— A step, a word, a voice, a look, —
    Alas! my dream is done!

And earth, and earth's debasing stain,
    Again is on my soul;
And I am but a nameless part
    Of a most worthless whole.

Why write I this? because my heart
   Towards the future springs,
That future where it loves to soar
   On more than eagle wings.

The present, it is but a speck
   In that eternal time,
In which my lost hopes find a home,
   My spirit knows its clime.

Oh! not myself, — for what am I? —
   The worthless and the weak,
Whose every thought of self should raise
   A blush to burn my cheek.

But song has touch'd my lips with fire.
   And made my heart a shrine;
For what, although alloy'd, debased,
   Is in itself divine.

I am myself but a vile link
   Amid life's weary chain;
But I have spoken hallow'd words,
   O do not say in vain!

My first, my last, my only wish,
   Say will my charmed chords
Wake to the morning light of fame,
   And breathe again my words?

Will the young maiden, when her tears
   Alone in moonlight shine —
Tears for the absent and the loved —
   Murmur some song of mine?

Will the pale youth by his dim lamp,
    Himself a dying flame,
From many an antique scroll beside,
    Choose that which bears my name?

Let music make less terrible
    The silence of the dead;
I care not, so my spirit last
    Long after life has fled.

我的孩子傑克

英國 魯德亞德·吉卜林 (1865-1936)

「有沒有我孩子傑克的音信？」
　　　海潮無言。
「他什麼時候可以回來？」
　　　　海潮緘默，海風徘徊。

「其他人有沒有他的消息？」
　　　海潮依然低頭不語。
沉沒了就不會浮起，
風颳不來，潮汐也無能為力。

「唉，天啦，我能找到什麼樣的安慰？」
　　　不會來自這波潮水，
　　　　也不會來自任何一次的潮汐，
唯一的是他沒有讓他的夥伴們蒙羞——
即使那麼樣的颱風、那麼樣的潮水。

請自豪地挺起胸抬起頭，
面對這波潮水，
面對每一次的潮汐；
因為他是你的兒子，
獻給了那一次颱風，那一次潮水！

註：傑克是吉卜林唯一的兒子，於 1915 年 9 月在剛剛參戰三週後陣亡。

My Boy Jack

Rudyard Kipling (1865-1936)

"Have you news of my boy Jack? "
Not this tide.
"When d'you think that he'll come back?"
Not with this wind blowing, and this tide.

"Has any one else had word of him?"
Not this tide.
For what is sunk will hardly swim,
Not with this wind blowing, and this tide.

"Oh, dear, what comfort can I find?"
None this tide,
Nor any tide,
Except he did not shame his kind—
Not even with that wind blowing, and that tide.

Then hold your head up all the more,
This tide,
And every tide;
Because he was the son you bore,
And gave to that wind blowing and that tide!

永葆童心

英國 威廉·華茲渥斯 (1770–1850)

每當見到天上的彩虹時
　我的心就會激動不已：
從童年時起我就是如此；
現在是成年人一點沒有改變；
即使我老了也要永葆童心，
　不然活著就毫無意義！
童真童趣是人一生的導師；
我希望我的日子是以自然的虔誠
將一天一天聯結在一起。

註：早前的英文詩常以第一行作為標題。譯者將標題寫成「永葆童心」可以更好地反映本詩的主題。

My Heart Leaps Up

William Wordsworth (1770–1850)

My heart leaps up when I behold
      A rainbow in the sky:
So was it when my life began;
So is it now I am a man;
So be it when I shall grow old,
      Or let me die!
The Child is father of the Man;
And I could wish my days to be
Bound each to each by natural piety.

每個早晨都是新的

美國 蘇珊·柯立芝 (1835-1905)

每一個早晨都是全新的世界。
你厭倦了罪業和悲傷，
這個時候是你的一個美好的希望 ─
是我的希望，也是你的希望。

過去的事情都已成為過去；
該做的已做，該哭的已哭泣。
昨天的過失留給昨天處理；
昨天的創口、受傷流的血淚，
夜晚已經將它治癒。

此刻：昨天已經歸於永遠之中，
它包羅了歡樂、悲傷與糟糕的時光，
一切都是上帝在掌控。
過去的日子不會再回訪，
無論是帶著鮮花或枯葉、
白天的滿滿陽光、還是夜晚的憂傷。

讓昨天過去吧：因為我們不能再來一次，
做過的無法抹去，也無法彌補；
上帝會仁慈地接受與寬恕！
只有新的日子屬於我們自己；
此刻的這一天是屬於我們的：僅僅今天的日子。

此刻：天空到處在閃閃發光，
此刻：消耗殆盡的大地重生，
此刻：疲倦的四肢充滿活力
面對朝陽，與早晨一起分享
沉浸在聖油般的露珠和黎明的涼爽。

每一天都是嶄新的起點：
呵，我的心靈，聆聽那福音合唱，
而且，儘管有往日的罪業和過去的哀傷，
以及可能的痛苦和預告的難題，
用心做好這一天，重新開始。

註：作者的原名是 Sarah Chauncey Woolsey。原文中的 the glad refrain 翻譯成「福音合唱」，因為 glad 有福音的含義，而 refrain or chorus 是副歌或合唱。

New Every Morning

Susan Coolidge (1835-1905)

Every morn is the world made new.
You who are weary of sorrow and sinning,
Here is a beautiful hope for you —
A hope for me and a hope for you.

All the past things are past and over;
The tasks are done and the tears are shed.
Yesterday's errors let yesterday cover;
Yesterday's wounds, which smarted and bled,
Are healed with the healing which night has shed.

Yesterday now is a part of forever,
Bound up in a sheaf, which God holds tight,
With glad days, and sad days, and bad days, which never
Shall visit us more with their bloom and their blight,
Their fulness of sunshine or sorrowful night.

Let them go, since we cannot re-live them,
Cannot undo and cannot atone;
God in his mercy receive, forgive them!
Only the new days are our own;
To-day is ours, and to-day alone.

Here are the skies all burnished brightly,
Here is the spent earth all re-born,
Here are the tired limbs springing lightly
To face the sun and to share with the morn
In the chrism of dew and the cool of dawn.

Every day is a fresh beginning;
Listen, my soul, to the glad refrain,
And, spite of old sorrow and older sinning,
And puzzles forecasted and possible pain,
Take heart with the day, and begin again.

觀刈麥

白居易（772 年—846 年）

田家少閒月，五月人倍忙。
夜來南風起，小麥覆隴黃。

婦姑荷簞食，童稚攜壺漿，
相隨餉田去，丁壯在南岡。
足蒸暑土氣，背灼炎天光，
力盡不知熱，但惜夏日長。

復有貧婦人，抱子在其旁，
右手秉遺穗，左臂懸敝筐。
聽其相顧言，聞者為悲傷。
家田輸稅盡，拾此充飢腸。

今我何功德，曾不事農桑。
吏祿三百石，歲晏有餘糧。
念此私自愧，盡日不能忘。

On The Wheat Harvesting

Bai Juyi

Peasants are busy all year long, and even busier in May: [1]
The hilly wheat field turns golden yellow
when southerly winds blow.

Women carrying meals in baskets, and children water jars,
walk in line to deliver food to men in the south hill fields.
Men's bare feet are burned by the burning ground,
and backs baked under the baking sun.
They seem to have ignored the heat though exhausted,
instead the long days of summer are cherished.

A poor woman is seen with a baby on her back
in the harvested field, a broken basket in her left hand,
she picks up some wheat left on the ground.
Everyone's sad when hearing her story:
She has to collect the leftover cereals to feed her family
'cause of the heavy taxes her own field has been sold to pay.

As I've never done any hard labour like peasants,
what merit do I have? As an official, I won't short on cash
since my annual salary is rather good. On my recollection
I feel ashamed and can never forget about this.

Footnote:

BAI Juyi (白居易 , 772–846), a renowned poet and government official in the Tang Dynasty.

(1) The lunar month in the Chinese calendar.

領悟、採納與體驗

印度 伽莉瑪

我學到的東西
經歷了艱辛的過程

習慣於經過曲折的途徑
探悉　因此我不擔心
接受結果的必然

在我看來　生活
不是彩虹和海市蜃樓
也不是滿園玫瑰

我已經解開了
被稱之為生命的謎語

我知道　什麼場合
應該掩飾自己的情感
什麼場合戒備要鬆散

我知道　什麼時侯
堅守　什麼時侯放手

我知道　何時何事
值不值得我嘗試

我知道　遇到什麼情勢
應該表現得成熟
或者要顯得幼稚

我懂得　什麼事情
會自發自主地做
什麼事情要退後一步
先想一想再說

我懂得　什麼時候作出反應
而什麼時候要保持沉默
我學會了相信　自己
頭腦裡面理智的聲音

我更知道　不必
為了無聊的事情爭爭吵吵

我更知道不衝動行事
以免犯錯後悔的道理

我更知道　絕對不要
為自己無法控制的東西煩惱

我曉得　一寸光陰一寸金
不花時間去做錯誤的事情

我曉得　往事如煙
讓過去消散在天邊

我學會了讓曾經的朋友
想離開的離開　而且
珍惜朋友們的留下來

我學會了欣賞　甚至
是生活中的小事　從內心
而不是外界獲得歡喜

我理解　世上沒有免費的午餐
一切都有代價　有的很重很慘

堅持用理性和良知
提高我自己的品質

我非常清楚　生活中
一定會有煩惱與憂愁

這是必須要學的東西
沒有任何的理由抗拒

生活中最好的老師
就是生活本身　它給最軟弱的心
講授最難懂的課程

這不是吹噓與誇誇其談

我知道　我只是一個少年
一雙充滿夢想的眼睛
一個充滿想法的大腦
相信超自然的魔力與神奇
正在找尋擺脫束縛的密徑

我理解　你讀到這些
可能會認為不值得一提
因為　比起其他的人
我缺乏人生的體驗

然而　有足夠的智慧
讓我知道什麼是對與錯
明白什麼有價值
值得堅持　雖然
我沒有體驗過太多的人生
但是　我有著自己的一份
失意與失落　清楚自己寫的什麼

這是一個漫長的旅途　但我知道
生命中還有很多很多的東西　需要探索
然而　這不就是生命的全部嗎？
領悟、採納與體驗！

註：這是一位印度中學生的散文詩。少年強，則國家強。少年思考，則國家難走
彎路。願所有的華人少年都勤於獨立之思考。

Realisation, Acceptance and Experience

Garima

I've learnt things
the hard way

I'm accustomed to
learning things the hard way
so I ain't afraid
to accept the inevitable

I've perceived life is neither
rainbows and unicorns
nor a bed of roses

I've unravelled
the enigma called life

I've learnt when
to mask my emotions
and when to let my guard down

I've learnt when
to stick around
and when to let go

I've learnt when
it's worth trying
and when not

I've learnt when
to act mature
and when childish

I've learnt when
to take a spontaneous action
and when to take a step back
and think before

I've learnt when to act
and when to stay silent

I've learnt to trust
the voice in my head

I know better than arguing and fighting
over something that's not worth it

I know better than acting on impulse
and regretting my mistakes later on

I know better than fretting
upon things I have no control on

I know how precious each moment is
and I've learnt to not spend it on the wrong ones

I've learnt to
let bygones be bygones

I've learnt to let those
who want to walk away go
and celebrate the ones that stay

I've learnt to appreciate even
the little things in life and
find happiness within not outside

I've realised nothing comes free in life
everything comes with a price
which can be really hefty sometimes

I've embellished myself
with consciousness and rationalism

I'm conscious of the distress
that life brings along

it's something we have to learn
no excuses entertained

and the best teacher in life is life itself
it teaches the hardest lessons
to the softest hearts

it ain't something to brag about

I know I'm none but a young teenager
having eyes filled with dreams
and head full of thoughts
believing in magic
finding my escape

I know when you read this
you might think it's rubbish
because I've no experience
in contrast of many others

but I'm sensible enough to
perceive what's right and wrong
realise what is valuable
worth holding onto
I may not have experienced much in life
but I've had my own share
of downfalls and breakdowns
to comprehend what I'm writing

it's been a long haul but I know
I'm still yet to discover much more in life

but isn't it what life is all about?
realisation, acceptance and experience

*~ **Garima** (The Wandering Writer) © 2021*
IG @_thewanderingwriter_ India

十一月四日風雨大作

陸遊，1192 年

僵臥孤村不自哀，
尚思為國戍輪台。
夜闌臥聽風吹雨，
鐵馬冰河入夢來。

Stormy Day, 4 November

LU You

No self pity while living in a remote valley
being poorly, and ponder relentlessly
how to defend my country.
In the night lying down in bed, surrounded
by the stormy sound, entered my dream the mighty cavalry
crossing frozen river charging forward.

Footnote:
This poem was written in 1192 by a famous poet LU You (陸游 , 1125 – 1210), the Southern Song Dynasty. Some Chinese netizens have wondered if he wrote this poem for Trump over 800 years ago —— what an imaginative and fascinating connection! Yes, 4 November 2020 was indeed a very stormy day in politics for the former US President Trump.

童年的味道

紅莧菜炒大蒜頭兮，
菜湯泡飯就成了紅米飯，
這曾是我童年難得的美味佳餚。
而今，在他鄉種植與享用
紅莧菜，紅米飯兮
故鄉的味道，依然在舌尖。
永遠不能釋懷兮，童年的味道。

Taste of Childhood

Red hsien tsai, Chinese spinach, or an edible amaranth
Stir-fried with garlic cloves is a delicious dish.
Soaked in its soup, the colour of cooked rice becomes red
Used to be a rare delicacy in my childhood.
Now I grow and enjoy eating them in a foreign place,
And the taste of my birthplace is the same in the red rice.
O! The taste of one's childhood one never forgets.

野天鵝

美國 艾薩克·麥克萊倫 (1806－1899)

哦，最具貴族氣質的鳥兒，你來自遠方
來自風雪經常肆虐的北極故鄉；
那裡，海象群棲息在浮冰層，
黑色的海豹們在滿是泡沫的冰水中翻滾：
白極熊悄然潛行在雪地上，
雪屋裡的愛斯基摩人在放聲歡唱；
這個深膚色的部落敢於衝浪在浪花之尖，
追殺獵物他們用的是長矛和弓箭。

飛越那伸展至遠方的雪茫茫大地
漂移的冰層上掠過你翅膀的影子。

在西方世界，你的群種幾近滅亡，
而很久以前，到處見到你的夥伴在空中飛翔，
一群群地出沒於湖泊、河流、大片的淺水灘
以及人跡罕至的水岸，美麗之景象令人難忘；
可如今，唉！你們成群結隊地遺棄了池塘
沼澤與湖泊，那些你們常去的老地方！

在過去的歲月裡，你的美麗曾讓世界著迷。
貴族富賈們，當構建優美造型的船隻時，(1)
他們會在你完美的體型中尋求完美，
精心模仿，塗上金色讓它閃亮華麗。
克麗奧佩脫拉就從這樣的精美之舟中走了出來 (2)
她曾經征服了安東尼並且統治了世界。

在遙遠的南方，有廣闊的環礁湖
陽光燦爛的島嶼、大群島
在白沙灘上佈滿水晶般的貝殼的地方，
每一塊長著金色果實的綠色空地都在發光；
那裡，高聳著棕櫚樹和木蘭，
美麗動人的小花兒像天空一樣燦爛。
你應該把家安在那常年盛開的花叢之中
大海與水岸看著你雪白的羽翼掠過上空。

註：
(1) 原英文中的 bark 或 barks，古老的文學用法指 ship/boat（船／舟）。
(2) 克麗奧佩脫拉（Cleopatra），華人也稱其為「埃及艷后」。

The Wild Swan

Isaac McLellan (1806 – 1899)

Far dost thou come, O bird of noblest form,
From stormy regions of the Arctic home;
From icy floes where walrus herds resort,
And the black seal-flocks tumble in the foam:
Where prowls the white bear o'er the icy fields,
And rise the snow huts of the Esquimaux;
Swart tribes are they who dare the frothy surf,
Pursuing victims with the spear and bow.

There o'er the drifting, far extending snows
The shadows of thy wings sweep o'er the floes.

In Western realms thy race is nigh extinct,
Realms where thy flocks once fill'd the air of yore,
Haunting the lakes and rivers in great flocks,
The great bayous and unfrequented shore;
But now, alas! thy swarming files forsake
Those ancient haunts in river, bog and lake!

In ages past thy beauty charm'd the world.
Great nobles, where their shapely barks were built,
Would seek perfection in thy perfect shape,
Modeled with skill, resplendent with their gilt.
In such fair bark went Cleopatra forth
To conquer Antony and rule the earth.

Far off in Southern haunt, in broad lagoon,
In sunny isles, grand archipelagos
Where the white sands with crystal shells are strewn,
And each green glade with golden fruitage glows;
Where soars the palm-trees and magnolias rise,
And gorgeous flowerets shine like brilliant skies.
There 'mid perennial blooms thy home shall be
Thy snowy pinions sweep o'er shore and sea.

Footnote: This is the version written by the speaker in 1896.

致水仙花

英國 羅伯特‧赫里克 (1591-1674)

美麗的水仙花兮，我們淚流哀傷
　　看著你離別得這樣匆忙；
初升的朝陽兮
　　未及晌午。
噫，何必如此倉促，
　　等到匆匆的白天兮
　　慢下腳步
　　等待晚禱之時；
我們一起頌唱兮，
　　然後與你一起離去。

我們只有短暫的時光兮，與你一樣，
　　我們的春天不長；
快速成長兮接著就是凋謝，
　　與你或其他事物一樣。
我們的死亡兮
　　如同你的來去匆忙，乾枯
　　消逝，
　　與夏日陣雨一樣；
或像清晨的露珠，
　　一去兮永久消失。

To Daffodils

Robert Herrick (1591-1674)

Fair Daffodils, we weep to see
  You haste away so soon;
As yet the early-rising sun
  Has not attain'd his noon.
Stay, stay,
  Until the hasting day
  Has run
  But to the even-song;
And, having pray'd together, we
  Will go with you along.

We have short time to stay, as you,
  We have as short a spring;
As quick a growth to meet decay,
  As you, or anything.
We die
  As your hours do, and dry
  Away,
  Like to the summer's rain;
Or as the pearls of morning's dew,
  Ne'er to be found again.

致露卡鷥塔：奔赴戰場前的告白

英國 理查德·洛夫萊斯 (1618－1657)

我心上的人，請別抱怨
　說我奔赴戰場是冷酷無情，
你彷彿生活在修道院
　擁有安寧而又純潔的心靈。

確實有一位新的情人，我正追著她，
　戰場上的第一個冤家；
一匹馬，一把利劍，一個盾牌
　我有更強的信念作為一名騎士歸來。

然而，我如此的見異思遷
　你也會愛慕與同情；
我親愛的人，請相信我的話，
　我對你的愛無以復加。

註：露卡鷥塔（Lucasta）是一個虛構的名字，源自拉丁語，意思是「純潔之光」。

To Lucasta, On Going to the Wars

Richard Lovelace (1618 – 1657)

Tell me not, Sweet, I am unkind,
    That from the nunnery
Of thy chaste breast and quiet mind
    To war and arms I fly.

True, a new mistress now I chase,
    The first foe in the field;
And with a stronger faith embrace
    A sword, a horse, a shield.

Yet this inconstancy is such
    As you too shall adore;
I could not love thee, Dear, so much,
    Lov'd I not honour more.

你是我的詩

孟加拉國 瑪塔卜·班加里

給我一些字
我把它們組成詞
給我一些詞
我寫成句
給我一些句子
我就作成詩
給我一些詩
我就會找到　你

這些　是對你的詩意的描繪
這個你是 — 詩的花蕾
詩的莖
詩的花瓣
詩的葉
你的芬芳　從庭院到庭院　傳播
從港口到港口 — 乃至整個宇宙
這個你　僅僅是詩的一根枝椏
而我　就是你多情的靈魂之鳥
經由充滿詩意的愛情
尋求牢不可破的戒指

You Are My Poem

Mahtab Bangalee

Give me some letters
I'll make words
Give me some words
I'll make sentence
Give me some sentences
I'll make poetry
Give me some poems
I'll find you there

This is all about your poetic denotations
This you are- the poetic buds,
The poetic stalks,
The poetic petals,
The poetic leaves.
And as the poetic fragrance
you spread from yard to yard,
From port to port - all throughout the cosmos.
And this you are only one poetic bough
Where I've come as your amorous bird of soul
And through the poetic love I seek impenetrable ring.

Mahtab Bangalee, Chattogram, Bangladesh
Copyright 2018, All Rights Reserved

青 春

美國 塞謬爾·厄爾曼 (1840-1924)

青春，
不是生命中的一段時光，
而是一種心態；
青春無關乎粉腮、紅唇和柔軟膝蓋，
而是人的意志力、豐富的想像力與情感的活力；
青春是清新和精力充沛的生命之泉。

青春的標記
是敢想敢幹的勇氣而不是儒弱膽怯，
敢於冒險而非貪圖安逸。
相比二十歲的青年，此膽識在花甲之男中更常見。
我們變老是因為放棄了理想，
而不是僅僅幾歲之年長。

歲月或許使皮膚起皺，但是
沒了激情會使精神頹廢。
不自信、憂慮和恐懼
會使人失魂落魄、意冷心灰。

無論是六十還是十六，
每個人心中都有對好奇的誘惑、
對未知的孩子般的飢渴，
以及對日常生活的樂趣。

你我的心底，
有一個無線接收器 —
只要能從有限的人間和無限的上帝那裡
收到美麗、希望、歡樂、勇氣和力量的信息，
青春之樹就會常綠。

一旦天線關閉，
意志被憤世嫉俗和悲觀失望的冰雪掩埋，
即使年方二十，也已經老衰；
然而，只要天線一直打開，
捕捉樂觀的電波，即使八十歲去世，
也是年輕地回歸上帝。

Youth

Samuel Ullman (1840 - 1924)

Youth is not a time of life; it is a state of mind; it is not a matter of rosy cheeks, red lips and supple knees; it is a matter of the will, a quality of the imagination, a vigor of the emotions; it is the freshness of the deep springs of life.

Youth means a temperamental predominance of courage over timidity of the appetite, for adventure over the love of ease. This often exists in a man of sixty more than a boy of twenty. Nobody grows old merely by a number of years. We grow old by deserting our ideals.

Years may wrinkle the skin, but to give up enthusiasm wrinkles the soul. Worry, fear, self-distrust bows the heart and turns the spirit back to dust.

Whether sixty or sixteen, there is in every human being's heart the lure of wonder, the unfailing child-like appetite of what's next, and the joy of the game of living. In the center of your heart and my heart there is a wireless station; so long as it receives messages of beauty, hope, cheer, courage and power from men and from the infinite, so long are you young.

When the aerials are down, and your spirit is covered with snows of cynicism and the ice of pessimism, then you are grown old, even at twenty, but as long as your aerials are up, to catch the waves of optimism, there is hope you may die young at eighty.

社會
Society

那位年輕的少女，當她的眼淚
　　獨自在月光下閃亮 —
她的淚為離去的和所愛的人流淌 —
　　會不會輕聲將我的詩歌吟唱？

Will the young maiden, when her tears
　　Alone in moonlight shine —
Tears for the absent and the loved —
　　Murmur some song of mine?

自由不會從天降

自由有價
乞求不能獲得它
不幸生在獨裁土地上的人
手足抗爭靠大家
昂首站立對專制
膝蓋有金絕不跪下

自由有價
法令也不能維持它
有幸生在民主社會的人
秉持正義尊紀守法
固守普世價值
悉心為它添磚加瓦

Freedom Not Free
— To all freedom fighters

Freedom isn't free
It can't be granted by plea
Those unfortunate people in a rogue regime
must all fight for it
and stand firm in the face of tyranny
Not to knee

Freedom isn't free
It can't be maintained by decree
Those fortunate people in a free country
must all stand up for law and order, and justice
and preserve the universal values
that can't be carefree

美麗之美國

美國 凱瑟琳·利·貝茲 (1859 – 1929)

呵，秀麗之國度兮，
高曠天穹，金色麥浪，
雄偉的紫色山脈，
浮現在肥沃豐碩的平原之上！
美國！美國！
上帝之恩典兮 ──
賦妳榮耀，予妳友朋。
灼灼大洋兮，從西到東！

呵，壯闊之信仰者征途兮，
威風凜凜，慷慨激昂，
隨著戰鼓咚咚，
沿著自由之路穿越洪荒！
美國！美國！
上帝之恩典兮 ──
補妳瑕疵，助妳自律。
自由之精神兮，法律保障！

呵，不朽之英烈證明兮，
獨立戰爭，愛國奉獻，
忘我之精神，
慈悲憐憫超過生命！
美國！美國！
上帝之恩典兮 —
煉妳真金，譽妳功成。
每一份收穫兮，高尚神聖！

呵，美麗的愛國者之夢兮，
洞見未來，歲月互久，
白色城市燦爛輝煌，
熱淚盈眶擁抱希望！
美國！美國！
上帝之恩典兮 —
賦妳榮耀，予妳友朋。
灼灼大洋兮，從西到東！

註：這是根據 1911 年的版本翻譯。

America the Beautiful

Katharine Lee Bates (1859 – 1929)

O beautiful for spacious skies,
For amber waves of grain,
For purple mountain majesties
Above the fruited plain!
America! America!
God shed His grace on thee
And crown thy good with brotherhood
From sea to shining sea!

O beautiful for pilgrim feet,
Whose stern, impassioned stress
A thoroughfare for freedom beat
Across the wilderness!
America! America!
God mend thine every flaw,
Confirm thy soul in self-control,
Thy liberty in law!

O beautiful for heroes proved
In liberating strife,
Who more than self their country loved
And mercy more than life!
America! America!
May God thy gold refine,
Till all success be nobleness,
And every gain divine!

O beautiful for patriot dream
That sees beyond the years
Thine alabaster cities gleam
Undimmed by human tears!
America! America!
God shed His grace on thee
And crown thy good with brotherhood
From sea to shining sea!

Footnote: This is the 1911 version.

美國 — 獻給妳，我的國家

美國 塞謬爾·弗朗西斯·史密斯 (1808 - 1895)

獻給妳，我的國家兮，
這片多情自由的土地，
我為妳放聲歌唱；
我祖先的居住地兮，
也是信仰者引以為榮的地方，
讓那自由的歌聲，
在每一處山谷迴蕩！

妳，我生長的國家兮，
這片崇尚自由的土地，
妳的名字我愛得心花怒放；
我愛妳的一切兮，
岩石、小溪、森林和教堂點綴的山崗；
我的心歡樂得劇烈跳動兮，
如在天堂。

讓音樂充滿的微風、
甜美自由的歌聲兮，
在樹木草叢中飄蕩；
喚醒普羅大眾；
萬口齊唱自由的夢想；
岩石也不要沉默兮，
自由的聲音亙古傳揚。

這片自由土地的創造者是妳，
我們祖先的上帝兮，
我們為妳虔誠地歌唱。
讓這片土地永遠光明兮，
一直閃耀神聖的自由之光；
祈求妳神威力量的保佑兮，
至高無上的上帝，我們的王。

America — My Country, 'Tis of Thee

Samuel Francis Smith (1808 – 1895)

My country, 'tis of thee,
Sweet land of liberty,
Of thee I sing;
Land where my fathers died,
Land of the pilgrims' pride,
From ev'ry mountainside
Let freedom ring!

My native country, thee,
Land of the noble free,
Thy name I love;
I love thy rocks and rills,
Thy woods and templed hills;
My heart with rapture thrills,
Like that above.

Let music swell the breeze,
And ring from all the trees
Sweet freedom's song;
Let mortal tongues awake;
Let all that breathe partake;
Let rocks their silence break,
The sound prolong.

Our fathers' God to Thee,
Author of liberty,
To Thee we sing.
Long may our land be bright,
With freedom's holy light,
Protect us by Thy might,
Great God our King!

美麗的烏克蘭，美麗的葵花

啊！葵花
開在海角天涯
哪裡有陽光
哪裡就有她
正直挺拔象徵烏克蘭
她是烏克蘭的國花

啊！葵花
烏克蘭人喜愛她
真誠、熱情、陽光
只有惡棍才會欺辱她
青春、活力、驕傲
文明世界人人把她誇

啊！葵花
神聖的基輔、克里米亞
自由和平的生活
絕不會從天上掉下
背向陰暗、朝陽、向日
自由的種子處處發芽

Beautiful Ukraine, Beautiful Sunflower

O! Sunflower
Flowers everywhere
She always blooms
Under the sun
Integrity and uprightness
Ukraine's symbol, the national flower

O! Sunflower
Ukrainians love her
Vivacious, zealous and sincere
Would only a villain bully her
Exuberance, youth and honour
One all the civilized will praise her

O! Sunflower
Sacred Kyiv and Crimea
The life of free and peaceful
From the sky will never fall
Turning towards the sun and never around
Seeds of free sprout in the free ground

白 紙

一張張白紙握在手中
你的目光堅毅　表情從容
中國人百年的夢　自由的夢
盡在無言中

一張張白紙舉在空中
你的無聲吶喊　我聽得懂
中國人百年的夢　自由的夢
盡在無言中

一張張白紙飄在空中
我的心在追隨　激情洶湧
中國人百年的夢　自由的夢
盡在無言中

Blank Papers

Blank papers holding in hands
Determination in your eyes
And calm expression on your face
The century-old dream of the Chinese
Dream to be free
Speaks the loudest in silence

Blank papers holding in the air
Your silent cry
That I can clearly hear
The century-old dream of the Chinese
Dream to be free
Speaks the loudest in silence

Blank papers floating in the air
My soul follows hard
With the strongest desire
The century-old dream of the Chinese
Dream to be free
Speaks the loudest in silence

自由需要維護和捍衛

美國 吉木·F·瓦格利

美國憲法和象徵自由的女神像，
我深愛著的這片土地與自由的旗幟！
做上帝的僕人吧，你會富有；但是
那些邪惡和愚昧之人必定遭殃。

歷史在重演，我們再一次見證
豺狼衝進肥沃的羊群。
莫名的恐懼，拒絕智慧和罔顧事實，
獵犬們又在發動攻擊！
剝奪其自由，是他們的戰鬥號令！
請和解吧；永遠都不要有人喪失性命！

那麼，為何救世主，這塊土地的上帝，
願意愛；作出犧牲，並且主持正義？
祂愛羊群，但是自由不會白給，
祂的贖罪；是祂的選擇；讓你我獲得自由！

祂締造了這個國家；一塊避難地，
歷史性的文件和標誌物；有著深遠的含義！
美國憲法和象徵自由的女神像，
我深愛著的這片土地與自由的旗幟！

Freedom Isn't Free

Jim F Wagley

Constitution and Statue of Liberty,
The land that I love and the flag of the free!
Serve the God of the land and prosper; you will,
But the wicked and foolish shall be swept off the hill.

We see again as history repeats,
The wolves descend on the prosperous sheep.
Many fears override wisdom and fact,
The hounds once again are on the attack!
Take away their freedoms is their battle cry!
Show appeasement; never should one have to die!

So why was the Savior; the God of the land,
Willing to love; to die and take a stand?
He loves the sheep and freedom isn't free,
His atonement; with choice; releases you and me!

He set up a nation; and a place of refuge,
Documents and symbols; implications huge!
Constitution and Statue of Liberty,
The land that I love and the flag of the free!

Footnote: This poem has been published in Shutterfly 5/10/2019

在法蘭德斯戰場

加拿大 約翰·麥克雷 (1872 - 1918)

在法蘭德斯戰場上，鮮紅的罌粟花絢麗開放
在十字架之間，一排排一行行
標記著我們的安息之處；在藍天之上
百靈鳥兒展翅高飛、依然勇敢地歌唱
可是難得聽見，當槍炮聲不絕耳旁

我們是逝者，當回到幾天前的時光
我們曾經活著：迎接過黎明曙光、送走夕陽
愛過人也被人愛，而現在我們就躺在
　　　法蘭德斯戰場

請與我們的敵人繼續戰鬥：
我們失血的雙手
　拋下的火炬，你們要高舉
如果辜負了失去生命的我們
我們魂將不安，儘管罌粟花會長在
　　　法蘭德斯戰場

In Flanders Fields

John McCrae (1872 – 1918)

In Flanders fields, the poppies blow
Between the crosses, row on row,
That mark our place; and in the sky
The larks, still bravely singing, fly
Scarce heard amid the guns below.

We are the dead. Short days ago
We lived, felt dawn, saw sunset glow,
Loved and were loved, and now we lie,
     In Flanders fields.

Take up our quarrel with the foe:
To you from failing hands we throw
  The torch; be yours to hold it high.
If ye break faith with us who die
We shall not sleep, though poppies grow
     In Flanders fields.

黨旗裹著的

作者的話：2017 年的網絡上，登出了一位中國大娘挑著用破舊的中共黨旗裹著的回收品。看到後，心情無法平靜，以詩為記。

黨旗裡兮
裹著的是人民日報與各種喉舌
報紙上的謊言兮
被說成了真理

黨旗裡兮
裹著的是政治正確的課本
課本上編造的歷史兮
被說成了真實

黨旗裡兮
裝滿了報紙課本與各種廢品
大娘擔著的真理兮，生活之艱辛
真實的廢品兮，大娘生活之來源

哦，親愛的母親兮
您終於明白：
黨旗是用來裝垃圾兮
黨旗本來就是垃圾

In The Party Flag's Sack

Preface: An internet photo in 2017 showed an old Chinese lady carried two sacks of recyclables using the torn CCP flags. This work is my recollection of it.

In the CCP flag's sack
People's Daily and party's mouths kept
Lies on papers
Taught as truth

In the CCP flag's sack
Textbooks written as politically correct
The faked history on books
Taught as facts

In the CCP flag's sack
Papers, books and recyclables had
The truth an old lady carries
The burden of people's lives
Those recyclables in the sack
The only source of her income got

O mother, you now realize
The CCP flag is only useful for holding trash
The CCP flag itself is a trash

津巴布韋的晚霞

津巴布韋 約翰·埃佩爾

譯者的話：讀這首詩，可以感到非洲大地上的春風，可以聞到茉莉撲鼻的芳香。
祝福津巴布韋人民。

當他們呼喊著自由
熏木的煙霧　混合著甜甜的灰塵
與茉莉的芳香——
青草　花崗石　羚羊骨——
聚集在手腕上

血的顏色變得鮮亮
灰暗的血色記憶——
當他們大聲唱的那支歌
在非洲大陸回蕩的時候　我熟悉

西班達曾經蹲在洗滌室外
邊擦家人的鞋子邊教我
我倆都穿著過於肥大的灰褐色褲子
光著脊梁　光著腳
他擦著　我將唾沫吐在鞋頭上

他擦著　我們唱著
「上帝保佑非洲
抬起她的頭 …」
一遍又一遍　直到八月的鳥兒
飛來一起唱

我意識到　今年八月
茉莉花盛開　熏木的煙霧
使得空氣凝固 ──
他們是如何呼喊自由
我是怎樣學會他們的歌

寫這首詩的時侯
我的孩子們蹲在身旁
持久的寒氣
把津巴布韋的晚霞
抹在他們的臉頰上

這也是孩子們的歌
我一遍一遍地教他們
直到疲勞的雙眼　被刺激得
淚水充盈　令人愉悅的煙霧
灰塵和茉莉的芳香

註：John Eppel 同意將中文標題改為 「津巴布韋的晚霞」。

Jasmine

John Eppel

When they cried freedom, when the sweet
mingling of woodsmoke and jasmine
with dust – grass, granite, antelope
bone – gathered into wrists which turned

light the colour of blood, darkness
a memory of the colour
of blood – when their voices lifted
that song and sent it echoing

across Africa, I knew it.
Sibanda had taught it to me,
polishing the family's shoes,
squatting outside the scullery

door. We both wore khaki trousers
many sizes too big; no shirt,
no shoes. I spat on the toecaps
while he brushed: and while he brushed

we sang: 'Nkosi sikelel'
iAfrika…' over and over
till the birds joined in. August birds.
'… Maluphakanisw' udumo lwayo …' [1]

It comes back to me, this August,
now that the jasmine is blooming
and the air is stilled by woodsmoke;
how they cried freedom, and how I

knew their song. A lingering chill
pinches Zimbabwean sunsets
into the cheeks of my children
squatting beside me as I write.

It is their song too. I teach it
to them, over and over, till
my tired eyes are pricked with tears
held back, sweet smoke, dust and jasmine

Footnote:
1. (Zulu) "God bless Africa ... Raise up her spirit."

John Eppel, Zimbabwe
Copyright 1995, All Rights Reserved
(First published in *"Sonata for Matabeleland"*)

邁旦

邁旦兮，今日之獨立廣場 [1]
基輔市中心兮，烏克蘭英雄聚集的地方
2013 年「燃燒的冬天」兮，「尊嚴革命」[2]
或曰「邁旦革命」兮、「烏克蘭革命」
捍衛自由兮，擺脫沙俄而融入歐洲大家庭

整整 93 天兮，一夜又一夜一日又一日
英勇的烏克蘭人站起來兮，追求自由的生活方式
專權的總統越鎮壓兮，越多的抗爭者加入
用生命的代價兮，將獨裁者趕出自由的土地
英雄的烏克蘭兮，捍衛自由可歌可泣

藍天下的向日葵兮，陽光、帥氣、美麗
英雄偉大的國土兮，飄揚著英雄的旗幟

註：
(1) 邁旦（Maidan），廣場也，音譯，取邁向光明之意。
(2)「燃燒的冬天（Winter on Fire）」紀錄片，可尋。

Maidan

Maidan, today's Euromaidan, or Independence Square
In the centre of Kyiv, where Ukrainian heroes
gathered and did a dare
Winter on Fire, in 2013, Dignity Revolution
Maidan Revolution Or Ukrainian Revolution, the same an affair
Of defending freedom, getting out of the Russian tyranny
And joining the European Community

For the 93 winter days long, night after night, day after day
Brave Ukrainians stood up to fight for, of free, the way
The more oppressive the former authoritarian president was
The more citizens came out to join the protest, regardless
With some terrible loss of lives, they've driven out
The former dictator and defended the land of free
The great Ukraine, the story of liberty defended by
Many brave hearts, both inspiring and tragic!

Sunflowers under the blue sky, strong, handsome and sunny
In the land of great heroes, the flag of heroism, flying high

一品紅

美國 麗莎·庫珀

在收割的壟行之間
彷彿是冬日玫瑰　天使下凡
搖曳著的火紅葉子
如同聖誕領帶

來自一個古老的傳說
一隊播撒神蹟的人馬
虔誠地饋贈與捨施
信徒　在讚美詩中受洗

血紅的色彩
好像祂心里流出的血液
一品紅的常綠葉子
正如無窮無盡的點滴奉獻

不管請求是多大多小
上帝會聽見　你膽怯的祈禱
耶穌誕生的鐘聲迴盪
保佑卑微的孩童平安成長

Poinsettia

Lisa Cooper

Amongst harvest rows
Belies winter rose
Sanguine foliage arise
Embody Christmas ties

Rumors longtime past
Lay claim to miracle cast
Bestowed lowly alms
Anointed by parish psalms

Pigments adorn bloodred
Signify whose heart bled
Poinsettia evergreen leave
Infinite tithes to receive

Of all things great and small
God heeds a timid call
Nativity bells merrily din
Blest tis humble urchin

*Lisa Cooper, also known as Poetessdarkly, USA
Copyright 2020, All Rights Reserved*

紅色罌粟花

美國 麗莎·庫珀

濛濛廣袤的綠草地
站立著無數紅色的天使
戰爭大戲在眼前迴放　那些
過去令人敬畏的時光

我們謙卑地低下頭
緬懷前人的奉獻　面對墓碑
注目　那些犧牲的英靈
在曾被戰火摧殘的土地上綻放

士兵的承諾　勇敢無畏
投入高尚而慘烈的戰鬥
罌粟花兒向逝去的勇士們致敬
祈禱的鐘聲為他們而鳴

這美麗的紅色海洋
是流血傷口上的榮光
陰沉灰暗的蒼穹之下
深紅的洋面泛起微微波浪

Poppies

Lisa Cooper

Misty meadows vastly reign
Vivid blush blest stain
Reverent times past
Resounded battles cast

Heads hung low, tis grave
Remembrance of lives gave
Abloom on war-torn fields
Long ago sacrifice yields

Brave t'was soldier's plight
Noble harrowing fight
For whom bell tolls
Poppies honor lost souls

Beauteous sea of red
Glorified on wounds bled
Ruby span gently sway
'Neath skies somber gray

*Lisa Cooper, also known as **Poetessdarkly**, USA*
Copyright 2020, All Rights Reserved

扎心的疼
— 獻給劉艷麗女仕

多想對你表白
可你的微信更新不再
看到你眼中的期待
可我遲遲才來

你的《疼》是扎心的痛 (1)
中國良心承受的重
耶穌被釘在十字架上
你的心滴血在毒菜的土壤

君呼喊時我不知
我呼喊時君被牢屏蔽
等待荊門崩塌時 (2)
獻上玫瑰花一支

註：
(1) 劉艷麗的詩《疼》登載在 https://www.chinesepen.org/blog/archives/96303
(2) 指荊門監獄

Punch in the Heart

— To Miss LIU Yanli

Long for telling you my deepest feelings
but your account was banned by the cowards
Seeing the eagerness in your eyes
so much regret for my missed chance

Your poem *Torture* pens the pain of a heart in bleeding
the weight that a human conscience has been enduring
The Sacred Heart of Jesus is on the cross
and your heart bleeds on the land under communists

I knew nothing when you called out
and when I come you were already locked up
Waiting for the prison gate opens
I shall present you a piece of blood-red rose

Footnote:
• Miss LIU Yanli (劉艷麗) is a human rights activist and political prisoner, charged for the so-called "public disturbance" by the Chinese regime, and held in prison. Her case may be found, in Chinese, on http://wqw2010.blogspot.com/2020/05/4.html

• My poem is the reflection and reaction to her last post in her WeChat account banned in China.

雨滴

英國 亨利·斯茂萊·薩森 (1890 - 1967)

下落的雨滴淅淅瀝瀝，
落在鮮血染紅的草地 —
它被猛烈纏鬥的夜戰踩躪，
宛如慈悲的上帝流下的淚滴，
進而，沖刷我們的罪業。

Raindrops

Henry Smalley Sarson (1890 - 1967)

Raindrops falling,
Falling on the reddened grass
Where through the night battle held full sway,
Like Tears of God that drop in pity, then pass
To wash our guilt away.

沉默是罪業

當一匹落單的斑馬被獅子攻擊時
群中的其它斑馬飛快逃離
而獅子靠近野豬時　豬群會反攻
保護弱者　態度不同
結果就不同

一個性侵犯之所以會橫行多年
往往因為不少被害者忍辱沉默退讓
等到有一位勇敢者站出來時
才跟著說　# 我也是 (#MeToo)　有點遲了
大片的傷害已經發生

不能等到父親保護住宅反抗強拆
自衛過失傷人而被死刑
不能等到母親捍衛權益上訪
而被警察黑社會滅口
不能等到丈夫維權被綁架被酷刑被黑牢
不能等到上大學的兒女莫名失蹤
不能等到肺吸滿工業粉塵變黑了　肯定遲了
遲了　很多時候會付出生命的代價

對著小偷小摸大喊
對著性侵犯大喊
對著非法執法大喊
對著世界大叫獨裁者又在洗腦製造真理了
對著世界大叫專制政權又在變相大外宣了
對著世界大叫流氓又在收買良心了
對著世界大叫共產黨就是納粹　共產主義就是法西斯
慶父不死　魯難未已

Silence Is A Crime

— To all human rights activists

When a stray zebra is attacked by lions
others in the herd flee at a full gallop
While a pack of wild boars are threatened
they'll launch a counter-attack to defend
their weak and young. With a different attitude
the outcome is different

That an evil abuser could commit crimes
over many years is often because some victims
have felt ashamed, kept quiet or given in
Only till a brave heart stands up in public
then many come out and shout #MeToo. It's a little late
as large scale damage has occurred

Don't wait till a father has been executed
for mistakenly killing a government demolisher of his home
Don't wait till a mother has been murdered by the police
and gangsters 'cause she defended her right and sought justice
Don't wait till a husband has been kidnapped,
tortured and secretly jailed
Don't wait till undergraduates have vanished
Don't wait till lungs have turned dark,
full of industrial dust. It's too late
as many lives have already or will be lost

Shout when encountering thieves or shoplifters
Shout when facing sex abusers
Shout when suffering from the illegal law enforcement
Tell the world when a tyranny state is fabricating facts
Tell the world when an autocratic regime
is pushing its hidden agendas
Tell the world when rich rogues are buying conscience
Tell the world communism is the worst form of fascism,
that's communist Nazi
The human sufferings continue
so long as the communazi is in existence

遊學吟

少年無悔懷理想
躊躇滿志去他鄉
求知解惑時日短
披荊斬棘路途長
情癡傾注故土雨
豪氣融化北國霜
幾十尋道風雨伴
電閃雷鳴作吟唱

註：讀一博友之詩後有感而作，以此自勉。

Studying Abroad

Fair youth, full of dreams, without regrets
Going abroad with ambitions
Time's short when acquiring knowledge and finding answers
But the road's long full of difficult challenges
Longing ardently for the soft rain of homeland
While with enthusiasm of melting the northerly frost
Decades of seeking truth, accompanied with stormy days
Singing and dancing in the thunder and lightning

Footnote: This is composed as a reflection after reading a blogger's poem.

自由的味道

還來得及
吃一吃台灣的鳳梨
趁紅色的魔爪還沒有踏上綠島
嘗一嘗自由的味道

還來得及
喝一喝澳洲的葡萄酒
趁共產法西斯還沒有控制全球
嘗一嘗自由的味道

還來得及
幫一幫香港的「黃色經濟」
趁中共還沒有把它封死
嘗一嘗自由的味道

還來得及
自由的人做著自由的事
捍衛自由　反擊共產法西斯
永不言棄　自由的味道

還來得及？
這是在關鍵時刻的世紀巨變
這是在隱形的第三次世界大決戰
假如還在酣睡不想甦醒！

Taste of Freedom

Still have time
to taste Taiwan pineapples
Before the red claws snatch the green island
taste of freedom

Still have time
to taste Australia wines
Before the communism controls the world
taste of freedom

Still have time
Help Hong Kong's "yellow economic circle"
Before the CCP finally blocks it
taste of freedom

Still have time
people of free must do things freely
We must defend freedom
fight against the communist fascism
and never give up the taste of freedom

Still have time?
This is a critical moment in this century
when unprecedented changes take place
We all are involved in the great duel
of invisible WWIII, and should open our eyes!

淚水如石

美國 麗莎·庫珀

冰塊融化在杯中的威士忌，
酒中的震盪波慢慢地退去。
氣人的沉默，厄運的逼近，
在心裡沉重的沮喪中共鳴。

曾經度過鹹澀的往日時光，
再加些鹽讓特奎拉酒穿腸。(1)
莫名的傷感憂愁深入骨髓。
在酒杯碰撞聲中尋覓安慰。

那琥珀色的液體淹沒了憂傷，
微笑畫在喜劇小丑的面具上。
將內心的想法像恥辱一樣隱藏，
不會有人來為這樣的行為擔當。

在音樂聲中再來一杯搖搖晃晃，(2)
在毫無知覺的迷霧裡持續受傷。
鐵石心腸，不讓情感外流，
直到你哭出的眼淚是石頭。

註：

(1) 特奎拉酒（tequila），墨西哥的一種烈性酒。
(2) hair 'o dog 的意思是「再喝一杯酒，或再來一巡」。

Tears of Stone

Lisa Cooper

Melting ice in a whiskey glass,
Oscillated rings slowly pass.
Maddening silence, impending doom,
Resonate in heart's heavy gloom.

Pickled by a briny past,
A bit 'o salt for tequila blast.
Melancholy to the very bone.
Finding comfort in a tinkly tone.

Sorrow drowned in amber cask,
Painted smile on Harlequin mask.
Hide notions like shame,
No one for to take blame.

Sway to music by hair 'o dog,
Keep hurt in oblivious fog.
Harden a heart, no feelings shown,
Till you cry tears of stone.

輕騎旅的攻擊

英國 阿爾弗雷德·丁尼生勳爵 (1809–1892)

一

半個里格，半個里格，

向前半個里格 (1)，

六百名騎士

　　全部進入了那個死亡之谷 (2)。

長官下了命令 「輕騎旅，前進！

向大炮陣地進攻！」

六百名騎士

　　踏進了那個死亡之谷。

二

「輕騎旅，前進！」

怎會有人沮喪、失望？

儘管士兵不知道

　　長官犯了愚蠢的錯誤。

　　他們無需回應，

　　他們不可質問，

　　他們只能戰鬥、付出生命。

　　六百名騎士

　　踏進了那個死亡之谷。

三

他們左邊的大炮，
他們右邊的大炮，
他們前面的大炮
　　迸發、炸得地動山搖；
在槍林彈雨之中，
他們勇猛地向前衝，
六百名騎士
　　衝進了死神之嘴，
　　衝進了地獄之口。

四

他們的軍刀出鞘、閃閃發光，
在空中舞動、寒光閃亮
砍向那裡的槍砲兵，
衝殺敵人的軍團，此刻
　　全世界為之震驚。
他們衝破了防線
　　掩沒在炮陣地煙霧的裡面；
俄羅斯和哥薩克的士兵
　　在軍刀的砍殺下翻滾
　　肢體分離。
然後他們退回來了，可是
　　少了六百名騎士。

五

他們左邊的大炮，
他們右邊的大炮，
他們前面的大炮
　　迸發、炸得地動山搖；
馬和英雄
　　一起倒在了槍林彈雨之中。
英勇格殺過的他們
穿過了死神之嘴，
從地獄之口返回，
那一切全部留在了那裡，
　　留下了六百名騎士。

六

他們的榮耀怎能被遺忘？
噫，他們的攻擊真的瘋狂！
　　全世界為之震驚。
他們的攻擊令人欽佩！
向輕騎旅致敬，
　　那六百名令人尊敬的騎士！

註：
(1) 里格（league）是歐洲和拉丁美洲一個古老的長度單位，等同於步行一小時的
　　距離，大約 5 公里。早已不再使用。
(2) 英國輕騎兵的攻擊發生在 1854 年 10 月 25 日，是克里米亞戰爭 *（the Crimean
　　War）中的巴拉克拉瓦之戰（The Battle of Balaclava）。這次戰鬥是由卡迪根勳
　　爵（Lord Cardigan）率領的輕騎旅對抗俄羅斯軍隊的一次失敗的軍事行動。死
　　亡之谷是指巴拉克拉瓦戰場上的山谷地帶。
(*) 克里米亞戰爭由俄羅斯發起，發生在 1853 年 10 月至 1856 年 2 月。一方是俄羅
　　斯，另一方則是英國、法國、奧斯曼帝國和皮埃蒙特 - 撒丁島的聯盟，結果是
　　俄羅斯被打敗了。

The Charge of the Light Brigade

Alfred, Lord Tennyson (1809-1892)

I

Half a league, half a league,
Half a league onward,
All in the valley of Death
   Rode the six hundred.
"Forward, the Light Brigade!
Charge for the guns!" he said.
Into the valley of Death
   Rode the six hundred.

II

"Forward, the Light Brigade!"
Was there a man dismayed?
Not though the soldier knew
   Someone had blundered.
   Theirs not to make reply,
   Theirs not to reason why,
   Theirs but to do and die.
   Into the valley of Death
   Rode the six hundred.

III

Cannon to right of them,
Cannon to left of them,
Cannon in front of them
   Volleyed and thundered;
Stormed at with shot and shell,
Boldly they rode and well,
Into the jaws of Death,
Into the mouth of hell
   Rode the six hundred.

IV

Flashed all their sabres bare,
Flashed as they turned in air
Sabring the gunners there,
Charging an army, while
　All the world wondered.
Plunged in the battery-smoke
Right through the line they broke;
Cossack and Russian
Reeled from the sabre stroke
　Shattered and sundered.
Then they rode back, but not
　Not the six hundred.

V

Cannon to right of them,
Cannon to left of them,
Cannon behind them
　Volleyed and thundered;
Stormed at with shot and shell,
While horse and hero fell.
They that had fought so well
Came through the jaws of Death,
Back from the mouth of hell,
All that was left of them,
　Left of six hundred.

VI

When can their glory fade?
O the wild charge they made!
　All the world wondered.
Honour the charge they made!
Honour the Light Brigade,
　Noble six hundred!

清晨的廣場

就在那個清晨
火點紅了雲
雲點燃了天空
天空染紅了廣場
廣場上女神手中的火炬
落地熄滅
天空回到了黑暗

註：有感於網友「紅樹林間語」之推文。

The Grand Square In An Early Morning
— To all freedom fighters

In that early chilly morning,
The cloud was ignited by fire,
The sky ignited by the cloud,
The square then dyed red by the sky.
The Goddess on the square dropped the torch
In her hands, caught by death.
The sky then returned to darkness

呆滯的眼睛

美國 韋切爾·林賽 (1879-1931)

不要扼殺年輕人的靈性、激情和愛好，
他們可以做離奇古怪的事，盡情地驕傲和自豪。
世界的一大罪惡是幼童們長大時變得平淡遲鈍，
而窮人們像牛一樣，疲憊的四肢和呆滯的眼神。

不是說他們不饑餓，而是饑餓得毫無夢想；
不是說他們不播種，而是他們難得有收穫；
不是說他們不奉獻，而是沒有神可以奉獻；
不是說他們不死亡，而是會像羊那樣死亡。

The Leaden-Eyed

Vachel Lindsay (1879-1931)

Let not young souls be smothered out before
They do quaint deeds and fully flaunt their pride.
It is the world's one crime its babes grow dull,
Its poor are ox-like, limp and leaden-eyed.

Not that they starve, but starve so dreamlessly;
Not that they sow, but that they seldom reap;
Not that they serve, but have no gods to serve;
Not that they die, but that they die like sheep.

炮彈

英國 亨利·斯茂萊·薩森 (1890 - 1967)

呼嘯著飛行的死神兮
　　咒厭阻抗它的空氣，
然後一頭栽在一座教堂邊，
　　已成廢墟的神聖之地。

科學的智囊，蠢蛋的銀子
　　鍛造了一個鋼鐵奴隸
用來殺人兮，徒勞的結局
　　卻是一個孩子的墳墓被掀起。

The Shell

Henry Smalley Sarson (1890 - 1967)

Shrieking its message the flying death
  Cursed the resisting air,
Then buried its nose by a battered church,
  A skeleton gaunt and bare.

The brains of science, the money of fools
  Had fashioned an iron slave
Destined to kill, yet the futile end
  Was a child's uprooted grave.

患病的玫瑰

英國 威廉‧布萊克 (1757 – 1827)

哦玫瑰　你患了病。
看那毛毛蟲　隱於無形，
在呼號的風暴之中
於漆黑的夜裡飛行，

它發現了在你的花壇裏
充滿了緋紅的歡愉：
它陰暗而不可告人的示愛
會將你純潔的生命毀壞。

註：普遍認為這是一首寓言詩，作者將「玫瑰」與「毛毛蟲」擬人化。

The Sick Rose

William Blake (1757 – 1827)

O Rose thou art sick,
The invisible worm
That flies in the night,
In the howling storm,

Has found out thy bed
Of crimson joy:
And his dark secret love
Does thy life destroy.

烏克蘭與臺灣

烏克蘭上空的硝煙
　　飄浮在臺灣人的眼前
臺灣伸出援助之手
　　烏克蘭人握得緊
　　自由世界看得見

葵花：背陰朝陽　堅毅挺拔
梅花：不怕嚴寒　無懼風吹雨打

面對「北極熊」的侵略擴張
　　烏克蘭人保家衛國挺身抵抗
對岸的「大熊貓」張牙舞爪
　　「黑熊」站起來不會彷徨
　　深信堅強的全民國防

基輔邁旦廣場上的聲聲吶喊
在臺北自由廣場上振盪迴旋

強大不是荒蕪的疆土遼闊
　　也不是愚昧的人口眾多
強大來自自由的生活方式
　　更來自民主制度的力量

烏克蘭與臺灣在自由之路上
　　肩並肩手挽手　走向陽光

Ukraine and Taiwan

The thick smoke over the Ukraine battlefields
    is floating in front of the eyes of Taiwanese
Taiwan lends a helping hand
    and Ukrainians hold tight
    and the free world has witnessed

Sunflower: always facing the sun, firm and upright
Winter-sweet: not afraid of icy cold, nor rain or wind

During the invasion of the "Polar Bear"
    Ukrainians stand up to defend their land
While the "Giant Panda" across the Taiwan Strait
    bares fangs and brandishes claws
    the "Black Bear" stands up without hesitation
    believing in a strong national defence

Rallying outcries on Maidan in Kyiv
are echoing on Taipei Liberty Square

Strength is not measured by barren and vast land
    nor by a large population of the uneducated
Power comes from the way of life, of free
    and more from the toughness of democratic system

Ukraine and Taiwan walk on the road of freedom
    shoulder to shoulder, hand in hand, towards a brighter future

女人與文明

美國 大主教 富爾頓·約翰·辛 (1895—1979)

在很大程度上，
一個社會的文明水準
取決於女性的修養。

如果男人真心愛女人，
他必須做到人格相當。
她的德性越好、
品格愈高尚、
對真理、正義、善良
追求得越積極，
男人就會越渴望
與她比翼飛翔。

實際上，人類的文明史
應該以女性的修養水準來度量。

註：標題為譯者所加。

Woman and Civilization

Ven. Archbishop Fulton John Sheen (1895-1979)

To a great extent,
the level of any civilization is
the level of it's womanhood.

When a man loves a woman,
he has to become worthy of her.
The higher her virtue,
the more her character,
the more devoted she is
to truth, justice, goodness,
the more a man has to aspire
to be worthy of her.

The history of civilization
could actually be written
in terms of the level of its women.

Footnote: The title is added by Yiyan Han

思與想
Think and Reflect

啊　思想者　在茫茫長夜
　　我多想看到你發光的羽翼
當你飛翔在天際時
　　我多想乘上你隱形的翅膀

O! thinker
I pine for seeing your glittering wings
　　in the long dark night, and climbing
on your invisible wings to fly with you

一語勝千言
—追念臺灣的「民主先生」李登輝總統

「臺灣交給你們了」
臺灣人熱愛臺灣
悉心建設臺灣
捍衛自由的臺灣

「臺灣交給你們了」
臺灣人享受自由的生活
亞洲自由的燈塔
拒絕中共的指染

「臺灣交給你們了」
呼喚臺灣的政治家和精英們
心懷臺灣、關注對岸、放眼世界
合力滅共、榮光歸民國

一個自由的中華民國聯邦
將是臺灣人世代安居樂業的根本保障
大陸人的期盼，還有澳門、香港
「西藏」、「內蒙」與「新疆」

三民主義 — 民族、民權、民生
聯邦政府 — 民有、民治、民享
「毋忘在莒」，目標正前方
聽，滅共的集結號已經吹響！

More Than a Thousand Words

— In memory of Taiwan's "Mr. Democracy" President Lee Teng-hui

"Taiwan is handed over to you" [1]
The Taiwanese love Taiwan
build it with their blood, sweat and tears
and defend their land of free

"Taiwan is handed over to you"
The Taiwanese enjoy the life of free
hold the Asia's beacon of freedom
and fend off the CCP's intrusion and interference

"Taiwan is handed over to you"
All of the Taiwan's politicians and elites are summoned
to keep Taiwan in your heart, pay attention
to what's going on across the strait and in the world
You must work together to help remove the CCP regime
and return glory to the Republic

The United States of the Republic of China, free and democratic
would be a fundamental guarantee for all the Taiwanese and Chinese
to live in peace and contentment for generations to come
This would also be the dream comes true for the Chinese,
and the people in Hong Kong, Macau, Tibet, "Inner Mongolia"
and "Xinjiang"
Three principles of the people:
National patriotism, civil rights, and people's livelihood

The future elected federal government:
Of the people, by the people, and for the people
"Never forget the mainland China"
where is still ruled by the commufascists [2]
and the rallying call is loud and clear that the CCP regime must
first be removed!

Footnote:
1. "Taiwan is handed over to you", the famous sentence by the late former President Lee Teng-hui (1923-2020) in a speech delivered in a 2012 presidential election rally of Tsai Ing-wen. He was often appraised as "Mr Democracy" in Taiwan.
2. "Never forget the mainland China", translated by the speaker from a Chinese idiom, 毋忘在莒 , which was used as a campaign title by the late former President Chiang Kai-shek (1887-1975).

因為他們可以

美國 魯道夫·約瑟夫·拉梅爾 教授 (1932-2014)

請告訴我，兄弟：
獨裁者為什麼要殺人
　　　並且發動戰爭？
是為了榮譽？為了財富，
　　　為了信仰、因為仇恨厭惡，
　　　還是為了權力？
是的，可還不止這些，
　　　因為他們可以為所欲為。

註：標題為譯者所加。

Because They Can

Prof. Rudolph Joseph Rummel (1932-2014)

Pray tell, my brother,
Why do dictators kill
    and make war?
Is it for glory; for things,
    for beliefs, for hatred,
    for power?
Yes, but more,
    because they can.

Footnote:
The title is added by Yiyan Han who has obtained permission to translate this piece from
https://www.hawaii.edu/powerkills/

笨拙的筆

如箭的目光啊
笨拙的筆
你為何能透穿紅塵
我卻無法寫下謎底

如風的言語啊
笨拙的筆
你為何能飄過城圍
我卻無法畫下圖紙

如電的思想啊
笨拙的筆
你為何能透擊謊言
我卻無法記錄無恥

Words of A Blunt Pencil

O! a pair of eagle eyes
You can see
What's going on in this world
But I can't write down clues

O! a stage whisper
You can be heard
Outside the Forbidden City
But I can't sketch the secret tunnel

O! smart brains
You can distinguish
Between facts and lies
But I can't record the disgrace

永恆

英國 威廉·布萊克（1757-1827）

貪婪於快樂的佔有
將難以享受起伏不定的人生

親吻人生旅途中的風景
生命的喜悅就如同朝陽之永恆

註：根據《每天一首詩》(*)，布萊克相信，是神聖的力量使他創作。神掌控著他
手中的鉛筆、刻刀和畫筆，而他僅僅是神的信使。

(*) Albery, Nicholas, Poem for the Day, The Natural Death Centre, 1997.

Eternity

William Blake (1757-1827)

He who binds to himself a joy
Does the winged life destroy
But he who kisses the joy as it flies
Lives in eternity's sunrise.

「自由花」嘆

— 讀陳毅《梅嶺三章》之〔三〕有感而發

陳帥泉台暝目嗎？
腥風血雨仍無涯。
革命理想如畫皮，
故土不見自由花！

Flower of Freedom

May the deceased Marshal Chen [1] rest in peace,
Yet the bloodshed in China still is endless!
Open eyes to the Communazi over the past hundred years,
Is there a piece of Chinese land where Freedom blooms?

Footnote:
1. Marshal Chen (1901-1972), a Chinese communist military commander and politician.
   This poem is a reflection on reading his Three Chapters of Meiling (3)

人類歷史上的大對決

我們正處在隱形的第三次世界大戰之中
新的冷戰　WWIII　即使你可能不認同
這是人類歷史上最大的對決　正確對荒謬
良善對邪惡　光明對黑暗　為了拯救
整個人類　每個人都必須選擇
只有選擇站在一邊　沒有中間綠地
沒有牆可騎　也沒有隨風的牆頭草
可以自由自得　逍遙

目前我們所處的這場最宏大的決戰
開始於 1989 年　在柏林牆倒塌之時
驚訝　不願意相信　亦或不解其意？
有形的柏林牆真的崩塌了　但是
隱形的柏林牆依然高高聳立　如斯
意識形態的卡位爭奪從未停止
東歐的共產主義政權垮臺了　前蘇聯
也解了體　看看地圖與這樣簡單的事實
地球上五分之一的人仍然被共產主義控制！

過去百年的人類思想體系的戰爭　持續
至今經歷了二個階段　顯而易見
1945 年戰勝了希特勒的法西斯
1989 年擊垮了前蘇聯領導的共產主義
然而　法西斯和共產主義的幽靈
在中共身上附體　演變成共產法西斯　今天
成了人類最大的威脅　這個合二為一的邪靈
是法西斯和共產主義的最凶殘的原形
在它的監獄中關著無數的社會良心

你應該反省　假如還認為共產法西斯離你很遠
或者相信它已經受到了很好的抑制
法西斯和共產主義　從它們出現的第一天起
就是反人類反自由反普世價值　一直
不遺餘力地在試圖搞垮世界自由的燈塔
偉大的美利堅　可是自由世界的黑暗勢力
幽靈政府　居然建設與中共的戰略合作關係
難道還會相信與參加中共的人類命運共同體？

你知道第一次世界大戰傷亡三千五百萬人
你知道第二次世界大戰傷亡七千萬人
可你知道嗎　從 1958 到 1960 年
至少有一千五百萬中國人餓死於大饑饉
在那風和日麗無大災的三年！
新聞告訴你　至少九千九百萬人感染
至少二百萬人死於武漢肺炎
可你知道嗎　從 1966 到 1976 年
二百萬左右的中國人死於非正常原因
那是中共黨魁毛澤東的「文化大革命」！
還有　你知道嗎？中共支持的紅色高棉
屠殺了大約四分之一的柬埔寨人
那是二百萬條生命！

你知道有多少中共特務生活在你的社區　以及
有多少中共代理人已經在跨國公司佔據了高階位置？
你知道有多少中共間諜在你的大學與研究所裡　以及
有多少中共特務活動在自媒體與社交平臺？　甚至
中共已經控制了不少聯合國的部門與滲透了多國的政府和議會！
醒來吧　不要再裝睡　這是關鍵的時刻：
人類歷史上的大對決　自由對決共產法西斯和黑暗勢力
沒有硝煙的第三次世界大戰　如火如荼在全球進行
我們必須捍衛讓人之所以為人的普世價值
我們必須用生命捍衛自由的生活方式！
這的確是一個關鍵時刻：不可戰勝的上帝
對決撒旦與一切妖魔怪異

註：文中的死亡數字均來自公開的資料。

Great Duel In Human History

We're deep in the invisible world war three
the new cold one, WWIII, even if you don't agree
It's the greatest duel in human history
of right against wrong, and good against bad
in order to save the whole humanity
Everyone must choose a side, and is choosing
as there's no middle ground, absolutely not

This greatest new battle has started at the moment
in 1989 when the Berlin Wall was demolished
Surprised, in denial, or even don't understand?
The visible Berlin Wall did come down, but
the invisible Berlin Wall still stands high indeed
The ideology battle of minds has never stopped
Communist regimes were overthrown in East Europe
and the former Soviet Union collapsed
Look at the world map and check on this very fact:
One fifth of the world's population lives in a communist state!

The ideology war of humanity in the past century,
on going even today
is rather easy to understand and no need to be weary
1945 was the year a war was won against fascism
1989 the victory against the Soviet communism
Yet the fascism and communism re-emerge as commufascism
in the communist China, the greatest threat to all of us as a human
The commufascism is the worst form of combination
You only need to count how many social consciences
have been prosecuted and are still in its prison

You do need to worry if you think the commufascism is far away
from you, or do you really believe it's already kept at bay?
You know WWI killed ~20 million
You know WWII killed ~80 million
Do you know from 1958 to 1960 in only 3 years at least 15 million
were starved to death in the great Chinese famine?
You've been told the malicious Wuhan virus has infected
more than 99 million
You've been told the deadly virus has killed
much more than two million
Do you know there were ~20 million abnormal deaths
in the 1966-76 CCP's cultural revolution? Besides
do you know a quarter of Cambodian population deaths
two million, were the victim of their CCP supported communists!

Do you know how many CCP's agents are in your community
and how many have occupied top positions
in some big tech companies?
Do you know how many CCP's spies in your research institutions
and universities
and how many lurking in social media and even in your society?
So please wake up if you're pretending to be asleep
This is the crucial moment in this greatest duel
of freedom against commufascism, the world war three
We must preserve all the things we treasure of universal values
We must defend at all costs our way of life, of freedom!
This is the key moment in this greatest duel
of our mighty God against Satan and its kowtow

Footnote: The statistics of death are from published articles on internet.

我們堅信不移，相信上帝
— 在絕望中不要放棄希望

在黑暗中我們渴望看到光明
在深水中我們渴望上帝的救贖
在幽靈政府的謊言中我們渴望知道真理
在失望中我們祈求上帝讓祂的子民幸福如意

你真的以為上帝不在觀看
你真的以為上帝不在聽著
你真的以為上帝不會願意
你真的以為上帝沒有寫下祂的神旨

問一問自己我們做過了什麼
問一問自己我們站在哪一邊
問一問自己我們什麼要懺悔
問一問自己我們是否要繼續

我們對上帝堅信不移即使在至暗時刻似乎見不到光明
我們對上帝忠貞不渝即使我們的小船似乎看不清航線

In God We Trust
— Hope for the unhopeful

In darkness we hope to see lights
In deep water we hope God will come to rescue
In the deep state lies we hope to know the truth
In desperation we hope God leads us to happiness

Do you really think God isn't watching
Do you really think God isn't listening
Do you really think God isn't planing
Do you really think God isn't willing

Ask ourselves what we've done
Ask ourselves which side we're on
Ask ourselves what has gone wrong
Ask ourselves will we carry on

In God we trust when it seems there is no light in the darkness
In God we believe when it seems we're making the wrong moves

無形的紅布

一塊無形的紅布
曾經蒙住了我的雙眼
它使我覺得是幸福

天安門是那樣的崇高
根正　甜水裡的紅苗
曾經是多麼的自豪

「三面紅旗」　東風在飄
思甜憶苦　西風被壓倒
與天地人斗　紅太陽高照

偉大舵手　指引航向
「破舊立新」　語錄歌唱
救星墜落　天塌般地嚎喪

總設計師揮揮手　「改革開放」
「四個現代化」　口號依然迷人響亮
「發展是硬道理」　我渡海漂洋

抹去了那塊無形的紅布
你問我的感覺是什麼
我說我再也不會有那樣的幸福

我要走　我有追求
我思念　我也會哭
因為我希望你也有真正的幸福

沒有了無形的紅布
你問我現在想的是什麼
我說我要為你爭取自由

我要寫　我也要探索
我有淚水　我也有歡樂
因為故土依然是那樣的熱

一塊無形的紅布
曾經蒙住了我的雙眼
它使我覺得是幸福

註：該詩歌創作於 2016 年初，受到崔健《一塊紅布》之啟發，作為回應。今作了一些修改後定稿。無形的紅布，泛指中共法西斯的洗腦與滲透。

Invisible Red Cloth

An invisible red cloth
blindfolded me once
It made me feel the happiness: —

Tian-an-men was so noble
Born in a Chinese peasant home
growing up under the red flag
how proud I was!

Three-red-banner the East-wind was blowing:
Recalling the past bitterness and appraising
then sweetness, and the West-wind was suppressed
Fighting against heaven, earth and human
the Red-sun was blazingly shining

The Great-helmsman dictated the course:
"Destroying the old and creating the new"
Mao's quotes everyone was singing
When the "saviour" died, howling as if the sky's falling

The Chief-designer waved: "reform and opening up"
The Four-modernization slogan then was charming
"Development is the last word" so I went abroad —

After removing that invisible red cloth
you ask me how I feel, I say never again I'll have
that kind of happiness

I want to leave, I have to search
I miss home and I cry too, because
I want you also to have true happiness

Without invisible red cloth, you ask me
what's on my mind at the moment
I say I'm fighting for your freedom

I want to write and I want to explore
I have tears and I also feel joyous
because the land of birth wants to be free

An invisible red cloth
blindfolded me once
It made me feel the happiness

Footnote:
- Red-sun/Great-helmsman/"saviour": In the CCP's propaganda, these were all used to address Mao Zedong, the CCP's supreme leader.
- Three-red-banner: Mao's so-called socialist construction movement during 1958-61
- East-wind: socialism; West-wind: capitalism.
- Chief-designer: In the CCP's propaganda, this was used to address Deng Xiaoping, the second CCP's supreme leader after Mao.
- Four-modernization: Deng's slogan for the modernization of industry, agriculture, science and technology.

把這一天留給自己

假如一年四季
只能做不得不做的事
那就在第五個季節
做些自己想做的

假如一年十二個月
只能說不得不說的話
那就在第十三個月
說些自己想說的

假如一周的七天
不能擁有自己的思想
那就在第八天
用腦子思考一下

在童話世界
《五月三十五日》： (1)
什麼都有可能發生的日子
把這一天留給自己

註：
(1) https://zh.wikipedia.org/zh-tw/5 月 35 日

Keep This Day to Yourself

If in the four seasons
can only do what has to be done
then in the fifth season
do whatever you want to do

If in the twelve months
can only speak what has to be said
then in the thirteenth month
say whatever you want to say

If in the seven days of a week
can't have a mind of your own
then on the eighth day
have your own mind

In the fairy tale world
of *The 35th of May*
the day when anything can happen
Keep this day to yourself

最後一撞

一堵退了色的紅牆
擋住了藍色的海洋

擋住了海子的理想 ——
面向大海　春暖花開 (1)

先輩們的綠地被奪走
青天白日被紅色淹沒
紅流所到之處 ——
高山低頭　河水讓路

先輩們長途跋涉
走過沙漠　走過荒蕪
走在貧瘠的土地 ——
走向希望的盡頭

今天我踏著先輩們的腳步
向著早已腐朽的紅牆
呵　擺好架勢 ——
鼓足勇氣　最後一撞

註：
(1) 海子：「面朝大海，春暖花開」

Last Push

A red high wall, faded and decaying
has been long blocking the blue ocean

blocking Haizi's dreams —
"Facing the Sea, with Spring Blossoms" [1]

The green land of our ancestors, taken away
The blue sky and bright sun, dyed red
Wherever the sanguine flood goes —
Mountains bow their heads, and rivers dry out

The ancestors had trekked
Through the desert, through the wilderness
And through the barrenness —
Towards the end of hope

We'd now follow the footsteps of our ancestors
Towards the already weakened red wall
Come on! Muster up the courage —
Ready, steady, last push

Footnote:
1. Haizi: the pen name of a well known Chinese poet ZHA Haisheng (1964-1989).
   Facing the Sea, with Spring Blossoms was one of his often quoted poems.

一念之差

一個人的一生中，某個或某幾個關鍵時刻，由於一念之差，錯過了機會，或做錯了一件事，後悔莫及。假如，這僅僅是一個人或一個家庭的事，造成損失或傷害的那是一個人或一個家庭的。但，一個人或一些人做的或做過的事情，關係到一個民族的未來和一個國家的長治久安，總該值得我們深思吧。

那一天，你站在高高的城樓上
說，我們從此站起來了，可我哪裡敢啊
你是站起來了，我只能趴著
本來，民主的會議協商
定下了民主的憲政大章
但你不屑一顧，棄之一旁
那個要命的關鍵時刻啊
智者的理論怎敵得過小人的捧場
再說，你手中有的是槍，還有
幾個死了的洋大鬍子作了你的排場
你的血液裡呀，帝王的細胞在增長
雖說不稱帝，換件新衣，可你骨子裡呀
要的是孤家寡人，權力至高無上
幾千年的宮藥啊，僅僅換了湯
自由民主的幌子打夠了
你把它扔回了大西洋
連同你「恰同學少年」的理想
這一念之差喲，千千萬萬的鮮血白白流淌

你想創造經濟的奇跡來證明一個幻想
煉鐵煉鋼，還有那三面紅旗飄揚
善良的百姓哪裡知道啊
他們的血汗，流進了狂人的痴想
人造的災難，有多少生靈去西天遊蕩
革命，口號是那麼的響亮
革命，你還沒有過癮
無數無知的熱血被你瞬間膨脹
整垮整死了多少幫你實現帝夢的老將
幾千年沉澱的優秀的文化文明啊
幾乎就毀在了你的手上
毛頭青年用過了，你指示他們
去接受再教育，上山下鄉
你該安息啦，因為你的軀殼
今天還有人排隊觀賞

那一天，你知道有多少人在翹望
撥亂反正，可什麼是正
回歸忠良，可什麼是忠什麼是良
被長期愚弄的百姓啊
好像看到了又一顆救星又一顆太陽
本該，重用被棄的自由民主的憲政大法
本該，重建綱常用來自大西洋的思想
可你要四個堅持，維護功成名就的故王
和那誰也搞不清楚的所謂的思想

這一念之差喲，你的被整死的戰友們
在西天氣得直跺腳，大喊大叫死得窩囊
那些為你抗爭於廣場的熱血心腸喲
被你灌滿了冰冷的陳湯
你知道發展是硬道理，知識就是力量
怎麼讓人覺得，那是為了太后的紅色衣裳
為什麼不敢要第五個現代化
難道就你一人文明
幾千年文明造就的百姓全都是豬羊
廣場的毛頭青年用過了，你指示他們
快快去蹲一蹲紅色的牢房
經濟好些了，上層建築卻垮了
你不讓一個再一個你黨的總書記改造破碎的瓦房
洋大鬍子的基本原理都不顧了
還談什麼主義，什麼思想
這難道不是天下最大的荒唐
多少年輕的生命喲，倒在那血腥的廣場
難道，難道，這就是你青年時的理想
你該安息啦，因為你摸過的那塊石頭
今天還有人在頂禮膜拜，在歌唱

那一天，你知道有多少人淚淌
你來到廣場，你說你來晚了
可孩子們哪裡知道你慈愛而無奈的心腸
那一雙雙童真的眼，緊緊地盯著你
難道你真的懊悔，真的絕望
難道你那隻百姓吃糧要找你的手臂揮不起來

難道你害怕坐你自己的黨為你備下的班房
難道你不知道 Nelson Mandela 可以是你心靈的夥伴
難道你不知道獨裁制度或遲或早的下場
這一念之差喲，你讓小人得了志更加的猖狂
自由民主抗爭的勇士們被關進了牢房
多少本該為國貢獻的精英，在異國他鄉流亡
本來，你可以寫下歷史，以總書記的身份
把你黨給你的牢底來坐穿
本來，你可以成為自由民主的先驅
你可以永遠是中華的好兒郎
你可以是百姓心中永遠不落的紫色太陽
天堂的你，怎能瞑目啊
大大小小的貪官污吏，久割又長
無數的百姓喲，病無所醫，老無所養
人災不斷，多少無辜的生命遭殃
哺育萬物的河川喲，污水在流淌
這一切的一切
難道你能安詳在天堂

啊，拷問靈魂的鞭子喲 (1)
重重地抽吧，噼哩啪啦地響
抽碎那宮廷的毒藥瓶
抽來民主自由的雨露陽光
抽去那獨裁者的謊言
抽出人之初的童真，追求真理的信仰
抽去邪念，惡念，帝王之念，一黨之念
抽來正義，慈善，民主理念，民富國強

啊，拷問靈魂的鞭子喲
你的節奏多麼激動人心
你的旋律多麼蕩氣迴腸
我祈禱
讓自由的歌聲吹到大地的每一個角落
讓民主的旗幟在每一個人的心中飄揚

註：
(1) 詩人尚飛鵬的「尋找拷問靈魂的鞭子」
https://www.poemhunter.com/poem/search-for-the-whip-of-soul-torturing/

Momentary Slip

In a person's life, at one or several critical moments, due to a momentary slip, he missed opportunities, or did something wrong, and then regretted it. Since the matter is personal, the damage will be limited. However, what a person does or has done something affects the future of a nation and the long-term stability of a country, this should be worthy of our thinking over.

On that day, you stood on the Tian-an-men gate tower
and declared that we stood up from then on, but how could I dare
You were standing up, I could only lie down
Initially, the consultations and meetings
of different parties before 1949
established the so-called "constitutional chapters of democracy" [1]
but you simply dismissed and cast it aside
At that critical moment, how could wise men's arguments
beat villains' flattery, besides you had guns in your hands
plus a few dead bearded foreign communists supported your cause
In your veins, the emperor's blood was flowing
and you were the de facto emperor with a new clothe
though you didn't claim to be
What you wanted was to grab the absolute power
and to be a supreme leader of communists.
The bottle of palace medicine of thousands of years,
only its decoction was changed
Even the pretence of liberal democracy
you threw it into the Pacific after taking power
together with those utopian ideals when you were young
O alas! The wrong direction you took in 1949 made the lost lives
of tens thousands of people were worthless!

You wanted to create an economic miracle
to prove yet another utopian fantasy: making iron and steel
by the population, under the three red banners
How could all the laypersons know that their blood,
sweat and tears
flew into the fantasy dreams of a mad man!
In the man-made great famine of three years, no one knows
how many souls of the dead were wandering around.
Revolution, the slogan was loud
Revolution, you hadn't done enough yet
Countless ignorant youths were instantly fooled
How many communist veterans who helped you realize
the dream of emperor were punished to death?
The great culture and history of civilization, accumulated
for thousands of years, were almost destroyed in your hands
After naive and young youths were used, you ordered them
to go to receive re-education in the rural
and poor mountainous areas
You should now rest in peace, for your face-lifted corpse
there're people today who are still queuing up to watch

Did you know how many people were looking forward to that day?
Setting things right after Mao's death
but no one seemed to know what is right
Returning to kindness, but no one seemed to know
what's kind and what's good. Because people who had been fooled
for a long time, and they seemed to see another saviour of China!
You should had adopted the "constitutional chapters
of democracy" abandoned by Mao, and started programs
of reconstruction using ideas across the Pacific
But you insisted the four persistences to protect the dead emperor
whose so-called thoughts that no one could understand

O alas! Your wrong moves had made many
of your comrades-in-arms of communists who were tortured
to death to stomp their feet in hell
Those passionate youths who fought for your comeback in 1976
in the Tian-an-men square were poured with cold water
over their heads
You declared that development is the last word
and knowledge was power
But your new slogans were just another red clothe worn
by the Empress Dowager Cixi
Why didn't you dare want the fifth modernization, of democracy
Were you the only one civilized, and the people
of thousands of years of civilization
all pigs and sheep in your eyes
The economy was getting better, but the superstructure collapsed
You even didn't allow the general secretary of your party
to repair and renovate the broken
and torn tile-roofed communist temple
You even ignored some basic principles of Marxism
What doctrines and ideas were you talking about?
Wasn't this the biggest absurdity in the world
The naive and young youths who supported you
in the square before were crashed to death
in the very same square, and no one knows how many!
Could it be, this was your ideal when you were young?
You should now rest in peace, as the stone you touched
there are people still worshipping today

Did you know how many people were in tears on that day
You came to the square, you said you were late
But how could naive and young youths know your kind
and helpless heart while their childlike eyes
were staring at you

Were you really remorseful, or genuinely desperate
Why couldn't you raise your fist to make changes,
together with the students
Were you afraid to be in the prison
made for you by your own party
Didn't you know Nelson Mandela could be one of your soulmates
Didn't you know that sooner or later was the end
of the tyrannous regime
O alas! Your timidness of doing nothing at the crucial moment
did let the villain to become more rampant,
and freedom fighters imprisoned
How many elites who should had stayed
in the country were exiled!
You could had written a new page in history, as a general secretary
who could eventually come out of the prison of your party
You could had been a political pioneer for liberal democracy
You could always be a proud son of China
You could forever be the purple sun
that never sets in people's hearts
You're now in heaven but how could you rest in peace?
Corrupt officials, big or small, come to power in succession
Still there is no treatment for the sick,
no support for the elderly, man-made disasters continue
to occur and countless lives are suffering
In rivers that feeds all beings, the sewage is flowing
Left all of these, how could you rest in peace?!

O! The whip of soul torturing [2]
please strike and beat hard and harder:
Smash that poison bottle of forbidden palace
and embrace the morning dew and sunshine of freedom
Expose the crimes and lies of tyranny,
and bring back the childlike innocence
in the beginning of human beings to pursue the truth

Get rid of the thoughts of red evil, of emperors, and of one party
welcome the ideas of justice, of fairness,
of freedom and democracy, and build a rich
and strong country of free
O! The whip of soul torturing, how exciting
is your rhythm, and how soul-stirring your melody.
And I pray:
Let the song of freedom sing in the every corner of the land
Let the flag of democracy fly in everyone's heart

Footnote:

The speaker tries to address to late Mao Zedong (1893-1976), Deng Xiaoping (1904-1997) and Zhao Ziyang (1919-2005), all communist leaders in modern China, respectively in the first, second, and third stanza.

1. For example, the article 4 of chapter 1 in the Guiding Principles of the Chinese People's Political Consultative Conference states: "The people of the People's Republic of China have the constitutional right to vote and the right to be elected."
2. Search for the Whip of Soul Torturing by Shang Feipeng, a Chinese poet
   https://www.poemhunter.com/poem/search-for-the-whip-of-soul-torturing/

不能，也不敢忘記

我曾在睡夢中陶醉
我常在睡夢中陶醉

那個清晨
惡夢將我驚醒
火光染紅了天
年輕的魂靈
與倒地的女神一起升起
美夢從那一刻消失
記憶的時針被折翅

為了我的女神
為了告慰年輕的靈魂
我不能在睡夢中陶醉
我不敢在睡夢中陶醉

Cannot, Dare Not Forget

I revelled in the slumbering state
I often revelled in the slumbering state

In that morning
a nightmare woke me up:
the sky above the square was reddened by fire
and many young souls
rose up with the fallen goddess.
From that moment the rosy dreams were shattered
and the hour hand of memory was broken

For my goddess
and for those young souls to be rest in peace
I cannot stay in the slumbering state
I dare not stay in the slumbering state

唯一之羔羊

英國 克里斯蒂娜·喬治娜·羅塞蒂 (1830 - 1894)

沒有別的羔羊兮，沒有別的名義，
沒有別的希望兮，無論在天堂或是人世，
沒有別的地方兮，可以隱藏我的內疚和羞恥，
沒有別的東西兮，除了你！

我的信念低落兮，希望渺小不足道；
惟有我的渴望兮，在心靈深處呼號：
我的憂傷和期盼，猶如隆隆滾動的沉雷，
向你祈求。

上帝呵，你就是生命兮，儘管我會死；
你就是愛的火焰兮，即使我寒磣無比：
我不在天堂，也無處休養生息，
更沒有家，但擁有你。

None other Lamb

Christina Georgina Rossetti (1830 - 1894)

None other Lamb, none other Name,
None other hope in Heav'n or earth or sea,
None other hiding place from guilt and shame,
None beside Thee!

My faith burns low, my hope burns low;
Only my heart's desire cries out in me
By the deep thunder of its want and woe,
Cries out to Thee.

Lord, Thou art Life, though I be dead;
Love's fire Thou art, however cold I be:
Nor Heav'n have I, nor place to lay my head,
Nor home, but Thee.

大地母親頌 （一）

澳大利亞 羅伯特·莫瑞·史密斯

親愛的大地母親啊　向你致以崇高的敬意
我們美麗的家園啊　只是宇宙中的小不點

浩瀚縹緲的上下空間
只見那點點繁星燦爛

太陽啊　送給你光明
月亮啊　與你結伴而行

你從遠古匆匆走來
一次撞擊帶來了永恆的風采

那天使般的小行星　以身相許
太量的爆炸　點起熔岩紅色的衝天火焰

讓你眼中的聖潔之水
滔滔而落　注成大洋湖泊

那江河溢出的涓涓細流
是你那甜酸苦辣的淚

讓第一批偉大的生命出現
走向每一片荒蕪

你昂著頭走過了冰世紀
跨越了火山　讓熔漿造地

你海納百川　讓數不盡的生命
生長壯大　代代繁衍

你無私奉獻棲息地給我們人類
以及那包羅萬象的大自然

你帶著萬事萬物一起環行
神聖的引力　無聲地唱著「縴夫的愛」晝夜向前

你不停地鑄造著山川　不辭勞辛
像那巨型的摩天之輪　從不休眠

可你的善良溫柔　卻遭受踩躪
甚至　來自那些你慷慨催化的生命

啊　大地母親 你永不停息地吐故納新
奔向神祕的未來　大步流星

註：這是史密斯先生 2017 年 11 月 8 日完成的版本之一。

Ode To The Earth (one)

Robert Murray Smith

the earth we salute you our dot
in space

nothing above, or below except
other lonely dots

shined on by a bright sun, and
a loon of moon

from eons you came alone, pounded
into submission

by asteroids red, explosive molten
flares

allowed your tears to pool as seas,
and lakes

rivers flooded, flowed streaming
anguished tears

allowing primitive life forms to
propagate

through ice, earthquakes, molten
moulding

you accommodated life in all forms
to grow, and prosper

a home for the whole of nature, and
finally man

all the while held in spins on spin
by gravitational pull

your moulding unfinished continues,
as you spin all alone

putting up resignedly to the desecration
of creatures spawned from your generosity

never resting always in flux into the uncertain
future you go

潘朵拉的錯？

幼稚　誘惑　好奇
哎呀　潘朵拉偷偷打開了盒子
虛偽　貪婪　荒淫　妒嫉
災害　疾病　饑荒　瘟疫
宙斯眨了一下眼睛　直至今日
人類的苦難啊　仍然在繼續

哪裡有永久的自由與正義
哪裡有免費的和平與安逸
哪裡有渴望的幸福與歡喜
希望中的絕望　還是
絕望中的希望　尋覓

撒旦力竭聲嘶
以均等的名義　推銷社會主義
看吧　在《一九八四》的中國大地
強徵　強拆　暴收　暴斂
以發展的名義
封城　隔離　堵門　監獄
以防疫的名義

黑夜　點一支蠟燭
祈禱　問一問上帝
可也　問一問自己
苦海中的孤舟啊　何從何去

希臘神話　是陶罐還是盒子
蓋子打開　鎖掉進了海底
潘朵拉沒有錯
我寧可相信她純潔的幼稚
人類　對　就是人類自己
到底為了什麼　違背上帝

註：「潘朵拉的盒子」，希臘神話。

Pandora's Fault?

Childish, temptation, or curious
O alas! Pandora stealthily opened the box:
Pretence, greed, debauchery, jealousy
Catastrophes, diseases, famines, plagues
Zeus only blinked his eyes, and till this day
The human suffering still continues

Where's the everlasting liberty and justice
Where's the peace and easiness, free of charge
Where's the desired joy and happiness
There's despair in hope
There's also hope in despair

Satan shouts itself hoarsely
To bootleg socialism in the name of equality
Look at the *Nineteen Eighty-Four* of China:
Expropriation, demolition, extortion, over-taxation
By force, in the name of development
Lockdown, gate blocking, isolation, prison
By force, in the name of epidemic prevention

Light a candle in the dark
Pray and ask God, and also ask ourselves
On the lonely boat in the sea of suffering
Where are we going

In the Greek myths, was it a pot or box
The lid was opened and the lock fell
Into the ocean. Pandora did nothing wrong
And I'd rather believe her pure childlikeness
Human beings, yes, the human beings themselves
have been betraying God, but for what purpose?

五顏六色之美

英國 傑拉德·曼萊·霍普金斯 (1844 – 1889)

世界多彩多姿，榮耀歸於上帝——
藍白相間的天空，好似地上的花斑奶牛；
點彩繪出的鱒魚，在水中盡情暢游；
秋落板栗如同火炭；鳥雀羽翼，色彩斑斕；
塊塊農田的景緻 ── 圈起的種植、新耕或休耕地；
還有那各行各業 ── 五花八門的材料、裝備和工具。

萬事萬物相反相成，原始、簡樸、或者奇異；
是無窮變幻，還是點點雀斑（誰能解釋？）
快、慢；酸、甜；眼花瞭亂、天昏地暗；
這都是衪創造的美，一成不變：讓我們讚美上帝！

Pied Beauty

Gerard Manley Hopkins (1844–1889)

Glory be to God for dappled things —
    For skies of couple-colour as a brinded cow;
    For rose-moles all in stipple upon trout that swim;
    Fresh-firecoal chestnut-falls; finches' wings;
    Landscape plotted and pieced — fold, fallow, and plough;
    And áll trádes, their gear and tackle and trim.

All things counter, original, spare, strange;
Whatever is fickle, freckled (who knows how?)
With swift, slow; sweet, sour; adazzle, dim;
He fathers-forth whose beauty is past change: Praise him.

輪迴

韋阿寶·雲鶴子，2017-11-14

曾經在那一世輪迴的渡口，
奈何橋上，
只為不把你遺忘，
孟婆湯只喝了一半。

多少個夢境裡，
依稀還記得你的容顏。

只為那遠古的盟誓，
我朝起焚香暮秉燭，
不為度己，
百轉千回只為修來世與你在娑婆的相遇。

Reincarnation

— A Chinese poem by WEI Abao

Once at the ferry port of reincarnation
on the bridge over the Acheron
only a sip of Lethe's water is taken
for you not to be forgotten

In so many dreams of mine
your face could faintly be seen

For the vow in ancient times, burning incense at dawn
and lighting up candles at sunset, it's not for my own
cultivation. To be reincarnated thousand times
is only preparing my next life for meeting you
in the Sahā world, on the earthly earth

鐵絲網後面的玫瑰

看著開放的玫瑰兮
鐵絲網飄來陣陣的涼氣
想到高牆內的那些玫瑰
觀花人不寒而慄

是玫瑰就要開放兮
鐵網內　高牆下　貧瘠的土地
不顧一切地開放
是玫瑰就要展示美麗

看著開放的玫瑰兮
涼氣裡透著涼氣
美麗裡透著美麗
玫瑰冷眼看著觀花人

曰：「你有觀賞的資格嗎？
我美在鐵網內　高牆下　貧瘠的土地」
無言以對兮　羞愧的觀花人
鐵網高牆外　生活安逸

Rose Behind the Razor Wire

Staring at a rose behind the razor wire
the watcher feels the drifting chilly air
Thinking of those roses behind the high wall
he shudders with fear

It blooms so long as it's a rose
inside the iron fence, behind the high wall
on the barren land, and blooms regardless
It always shows off its beauty so long as it's a rose

Staring at the blooming rose
the watcher feels chilly from the chilly air
and senses beauty within the beauty
Yet the rose looks back with cold eyes

and says: "Are you qualified to watch?
My beauty is inside the iron fence,
behind the high wall, and on the barren land."
O alas! Speechless! The ashamed watcher lives
a comfy life outside the iron fence ......

唏噓不已

屈原投江兮，不與奴才為伍！
魯迅已故兮，莫言乎坐牢乎？
故人西去兮，難斷其功過。
夭朝當日兮，少見人直立！

惟民國人傑兮，始華夏之復興。
惟國父中山兮，翻出新一頁。
惟蔣先總統兮，一手定坤乾；
惟經國先生兮，啓民主憲政橋。

我沒有敵人兮，為何滅其肉體？
捌玖之陸肆兮，天使魔鬼相遇。
柒零玖志仕兮，吾人之楷模；
高氏智晟君兮，九州之脊椎。

願神傳方塊字兮，去妖又降紅魔。
願正義之聲音兮，眾口放喉高歌。
願上帝之恒愛兮，流淌揚子黃河。

Sigh Of Sorrow

— China's sorrow

Jumping into the river, QU Yuan committed suicide,
despaired of the henchmen indeed!
LU Xun died early due to illness, otherwise,
had he shut up or been arrested as other dissidents?
Impossible to judge their right or wrong
as they passed away long and gone.
In the today's tyranny state,
few men are able to stand up straight.

O! Those great heroes in the Republic
glory to the country, in their time, have brought.
O! SUN Yat-sen, the father of the Republic
opened a new chapter in an ancient book.
O! CHIANG Kai-shek, the late president
to win in the second world war led the Republic
O! The president CHIANG junior had opened a bridge
of freedom and made it possible for Taiwan to be a land of free.

"I don't have enemy", once said a famous Chinese man
Why had he still been brutally murdered then?
On the 4th Day of June, Nineteen Eighty Nine
on the world stage shown angels and devils were battling.
Ode to the "709" human rights lawyers and their families
in China as they are truly brave human beings.
Ode to GAO Zhisheng, the dissident, human rights attorney,
one of the freedom leaders in the past century.

May the words, made of the God given block characters
force the red devils to surrender and expel the communazi!
May the voice of fairness and justice
loud and clear, be spoken out by all citizens!
May God's eternal love be forever flowing
in the Yellow River and Yangtze!

Footnote:
- QU Yuan, a famous poet, c.340-278 BC
- LU Xun, a well-known Chinese writer, 1881-1936
- SUN Yat-sen, CHIANG Kai-shek and CHIANG junior are all former presidents of the Republic of China, now in Taiwan.
- "709", known as the 709 Crackdown, a mass arrest of human rights lawyers by the CCP regime on 9 July 2015.

林肯的蓋茲堡演說

布利斯版本 [1]

譯者的話：1863 年 11 月 19 日，美國第 16 任總統亞伯拉罕·林肯在蓋茲堡國家公墓揭幕式上的演說，其背景是 1861 至 1865 年間的美國歷史上最大規模的內戰，通常稱為南北戰爭 [2]。那場大內戰的結果，維持了美國聯邦（即美利堅合眾國），並且廢止了奴隸制度。2020 年大選後的今天，選舉作弊的嚴重問題依然沒有得到解決，而且，美國事實上正處於一場看不見硝煙的大決戰之中：崇尚自由的保守主義對抗主張大政府的社會主義。因此，重溫林肯最著名的蓋茲堡演說，有鮮明的現實意義和深刻的歷史意義。故嘗試翻譯，並以此獻給所有追求自由和正義的勇敢的愛國者們。

我們的祖先　八十七年前
在這一塊土地上　建立起
一個嶄新的國家　她
生來具有自由的基因　並且堅信
上帝　人人生而平等

今天　這一場大內戰
考驗著我們這個國家　或者
任何其他有著同樣基因和信仰之民族
能否亙久長存

我們　在這宏大的戰場上相遇
我們　獻出戰場的一份土地
讓犧牲了的人在此安息
他們在這裡付出了生命
使這個國家的生存有繼續的可能

這是完全的正當合適
我們必須這樣做　可是
從更廣泛的意義上說
我們難以更多地犧牲 —
我們難以更多地祀祭 —
我們難以更多地神化 — 這一份土地

勇敢無畏的人　無論是活著的和還是已經去世
曾經在此努力拼搏　早已讓它神聖了
這遠遠地超過我們微弱的力量　是否讚譽或貶低

世界幾乎不會注意
我們今天的言辭　也不會永存記憶
但是　絕對不會忘記他們的事跡
恰恰是我們這些活著的人　在這裡
致力於先輩們偉大而崇高的事業
他們為之奮鬥　壯志未酬

恰恰是我們這些活著的人　在這裡
投身於擺在我們面前的偉大的事業 —
從他們光榮獻生的精神　我們獲得更大的熱忱
為了自由　他們奉獻了他們的所有 —

我們在這裡　下定決心
絕不讓他們白白地付出了生命 —
這個國家　有上帝的庇佑
一定會獲得新生的自由 —
一個為民所有的政府
為民所治
為民所享
永遠不會從地球上消失

亞伯拉罕‧林肯
1863 年 11 月 19 日

註：
(1) 幾個版本中，布利斯版本是林肯唯一署名的。
　　https://zh.wikipedia.org/zh-tw/ 蓋茲堡演說
　　在華盛頓林肯紀念堂牆上的，正是這篇布利斯版本。
　　http://www.abrahamlincolnonline.org/lincoln/speeches/gettysburg.htm
　　以散文詩歌的形式寫出和朗誦林肯這篇經典的演說，更具感染力。
　　https://www.youtube.com/watch?v=bC4kQ2-kHZE
(2) 南北戰爭（美國內戰）https://zh.wikipedia.org/zh-tw/ 南北戰爭

The Gettysburg Address

(Bliss Copy)

Four score and seven years ago
our fathers brought forth on this continent,
a new nation, conceived in Liberty,
and dedicated to the proposition
that all men are created equal.

Now we are engaged in a great civil war,
testing whether that nation,
or any nation so conceived and so dedicated,
can long endure.

We are met on a great battle-field of that war.
We have come to dedicate a portion of that field,
as a final resting place for those
who here gave their lives
that that nation might live.

It is altogether fitting and proper
that we should do this.
But, in a larger sense,
we can not dedicate —
we can not consecrate —
we can not hallow — this ground.

The brave men, living and dead,
who struggled here, have consecrated it,
far above our poor power to add or detract.

The world will little note,
nor long remember what we say here,
but it can never forget what they did here.
It is for us the living, rather, to be dedicated here
to the unfinished work which they who fought here
have thus far so nobly advanced.

It is rather for us to be here dedicated
to the great task remaining before us —
that from these honored dead we take increased
devotion to that cause for which they gave
the last full measure of devotion —
that we here highly resolve that these dead
shall not have died in vain —
that this nation, under God,
shall have a new birth of freedom —
and that government of the people,
by the people,
for the people,
shall not perish from the earth.

Abraham Lincoln
November 19, 1863

Footnote:
This Lincoln's classic speech in poem is much more appealing —
https://www.youtube.com/watch?v=bC4kQ2-kHZE

被劫持的地球

瘟疫　戰爭　饑荒　乃至死亡
似乎已經進入文明的人類
依然處在時代的蠻荒！
看不見的武漢冠狀病毒
2019 年以來的人類必須分享；
共產主義與法西斯的世紀幽靈
依然遊蕩在東方與西方！

1945 年被釘在恥辱柱上的法西斯
被披上了共產主義的外衣
也被裝飾了北極熊的「民選」毛皮！
1989 年血腥的天安門廣場
以及倒塌的柏林牆
被中共法西斯搬到了香港 ──
自由世界的人們必須觀賞！

共產法西斯反人類的罪行一樁樁　一件件：
烏克蘭大饑荒關聯著中國的大饑荒
無數平民死於共產主義的「天堂」；
蘇共、紅色高棉與中共法西斯
對人民的鎮壓和屠殺是它們的共性！
沙俄法西斯在烏克蘭大地上燃起的硝煙
是中共法西斯霸權夢中的碎碎念。

如果依然容忍共產法西斯，
地球上的人類還能僥倖存在幾天？

The Hijacked Earth

Plague, war, famine, and death
of the mankind which claims to be civilized
show that we still live in the era of savage wildness!
The invisible CCP Wuhan virus
must be shared from 2019 by the world population;
The ghosts of communism and fascism
in East and West, are still wandering!

The fascism in 1945, nailed to the pillar of shame
is cloaked in the cloak of communism
and adorned also with the polar bear's "election" fur!
The bloody Tian-an-men Square
and the fallen Berlin Wall, in 1989
have now been installed in Hong Kong —
People of the free world, as usual, carry on!

Commufascist's crimes against humanity one by one:
The Holodomor in Soviet Ukraine reoccurred
as the Great Chinese Famine
and countless civilians died in the communist "heaven";
The suppression and massacre of its people is the commonality
of the Soviet communists, the Khmer Rouge and the CCP fascists!
The gunfire of Russian fascists, started on February 24th, 2022
in Ukraine is reoccurring in the CCP's dream of fascist hegemony

If the commufascism is still tolerated
how long can the free and democratic systems survive?

夜有千雙眼

英國 弗朗西斯·威廉·鮑迪昂 （1852-1921）

夜的眼睛有千雙
白天只要一個太陽：
沒了它
世界就沒了光亮

大腦有千個慾望
愛是心中唯一之想：
沒了它
生命就沒了光芒

The Night Has A Thousand Eyes

Francis William Bourdillon (1852 - 1921)

The night has a thousand eyes,
And the day but one;
Yet the light of the bright world dies
With the dying sun.

The mind has a thousand eyes,
And the heart but one:
Yet the light of a whole life dies
When love is done.

星光之夜

英國 傑拉德·曼萊·霍普金斯 (1844－1889)

看看那些星星吧！仰望今夜的天空，專心地瞭望！
　　哦，看看所有懸在天上的火精靈！
　　那些圓形的城堡，那些璀璨的城邑！
就像在昏暗的森林中搜尋鑽石！還有精靈們的眼睛！
在灰色寒冷的草坪上有珍貴的寶藏，也有水星！(1)
　　風中跳動的銀白色光！閃爍的葉子搖曳在白楊樹上！(2)
　　就像受了驚的雪花般的白鴿在農家院子裏飄蕩！(3)
啊，好吧！所有的這些都是一種購買，都是一種獎賞。

買吧！報價吧！─什麼標價？─ 祈禱、忍耐、布施、發誓。
看看，再看看：五月爭妍，就像花團錦簇的果樹枝！(4)
　　看吧！三月綻放，就像黃色山羊柳上的雄性柳絮！(5)
這些的確都屬於穀倉；一堆堆一層層的麥子
　　儲存在裏面。這木柵欄牆透出的耀眼的聖潔之光
　　守護著基督伴侶們的家、耶穌與聖母、以及祂所有的聖器。

註：

(1)「昏暗的森林」和「灰色寒冷的草坪」隱喻空曠的夜空。而詩中的 gold 隱喻珍貴礦物，quickgold 意指 quicksilver (mercury 水銀)，而 Mercury 就是我們太陽系中的水星！仰望星空就是在搜尋寶藏。

(2) 從遠處看，白楊樹 (abeles，white poplar) 上似乎落滿了雪花，因為樹葉的背面是銀白色的。

(3)「跳動的白光」「閃爍的葉子」「雪花般的白鴿」都是用來隱喻星星。

(4) 根據《每天一首詩(*)》中的註解，「花團」與「花絮」依然隱喻星星。馬太福音 (Matthew 13:30) 中收穫的「麥子」隱喻天堂中的靈魂。而詩中的「穀倉」形象地暗示著耶穌誕生。就神學而言，基督的信徒即基督的伴侶。詩中的「家」隱喻天堂，「麥子」也包括星星在內，所以，閃亮的「星星」正是代表了一個個天堂中的靈魂。

(5) 參見 (*) 書中的註解，「黃色山羊柳」 (sallow, goat willow)，學名 Salix caprea。「雄性柳絮」英文 (atkins)，形如渾身長滿觸鬚的球狀海葵。

(*) Albery, Nicholas, Poem for the Day, The Natural Death Centre, 1997.

The Starlight Night

Gerard Manley Hopkins (1844 – 1889)

Look at the stars! look, look up at the skies!
    O look at all the fire-folk sitting in the air!
    The bright boroughs, the circle-citadels there!
Down in dim woods the diamond delves! the elves'-eyes!
The grey lawns cold where gold, where quickgold lies!
    Wind-beat whitebeam! airy abeles set on a flare!
    Flake-doves sent floating forth at a farmyard scare!
Ah well! it is all a purchase, all is a prize.

Buy then! bid then! — What? — Prayer, patience, alms, vows.
Look, look: a May-mess, like on orchard boughs!
    Look! March-bloom, like on mealed-with-yellow sallows!
These are indeed the barn; withindoors house
    The shocks. This piece-bright paling shuts the spouse
    Christ home, Christ and his mother and all his hallows.

聖誕之思

耶穌降臨人間　承受人類的苦難
上帝派自己的兒子　背負人類的罪孽

誰反對聖誕　誰就沒有人的尊嚴
誰反對聖誕　誰心裡就是醜陋就有惡靈
即使是沉魚落雁羞花閉月的美人也是白骨
即使是滿腹經綸飽讀詩書的夫子也是骷髏

聖誕的日子　是人反省的日子
有多少原罪沒有坦白
有多少惡行沒有清算
向上帝懺悔吧　祈求袘的寬恕
向上帝懺悔吧　祈求袘的恩典
點上一根心燭　照亮心中的黑暗

聖誕的日子　是傳播愛的日子
無論強壯軟弱富貴貧賤
無論男女老幼黃褐黑白
愛與被愛　每一個人的權利
將上帝的愛傳給他們吧
即使他們沒有信仰
金錢再多也可能是精神乞丐
生無分文也可能是貴族
上帝賦予我們信仰

聖誕的日子　是祈禱的日子
在平安夜祈禱平安
在聖誕日感恩上帝
感恩耶穌降臨與我們並肩
祈禱上帝給我們力量度過苦難
點燃火炬戰勝邪惡與黑暗
想一想我們做了多少
問一問我們還要做什麼
順著上帝的大手筆
挺胸抬頭　迎接新的一天

註：祝為真相護航為沉默發聲的大紀元和新唐人的全體同仁聖誕快樂！

Think of Christmas

Jesus came to the earthly earth
to bear the sufferings of humanity
God sent His son to die
a substitution for all mankind guilty

Whoever opposes Christmas is one
Without human dignity
but with a devil's heart
No matter if one is a celebrity
or has a sexy model body

Christmas is a good time for whipping one's soul
How much sins need to be confessed once 'n' for all
How much evil ideas one has to expel
O! Confess to God, ask for His mercy
O! Confess to God, ask for His love to be happy
Light up a candle in the heart to banish darkness inside

Christmas is a good time for spreading love to everyone
whether rich, poor; weak, strong; old and young
whatever the colour: black, white, or brown
The right to love or be loved each one
O! Spread God's love to those
who even if ain't Christians
One with money can be a beggar of spiritual needs
One without a penny can be of blue blood spiritually
God gives faith to everyone everyday

Christmas is a good time for praying
Pray for peace on the Eve, and praise God on the Day
Thank the coming of Jesus!
Ask for His mighty power in difficult times
to light up the beacon of justice, and burn off darkness
to fight against devils in the deep state and rogue regimes
What have we done? How long can we go on?
Following God's Light, we stand up on our mettle
and embrace a new day that's being born

思想者的隱形翅膀

思想　是思想者的隱形翅膀
什麼都可以奪走
什麼都可以放棄
什麼都可以忘記
唯一不能失去的　是他的思想
這是他生命的全部意義

思想者　小我小愛必須放棄
在大我大愛中　想和思
思想者　在文明與野蠻的搏鬥中角力
在民主與獨裁的交鋒中呼號
思想者　行走於天地間　漫步於生死線上
為了人類的終極之謎而苦思冥想

在嚴冬　思想者思考著春的到來
在陽春　思想者思考著冬的徘徊
在漆黑的長夜　思考著黎明
在陽光下　思考著夜的陰影
在野蠻的角落　思考著文明
在文明中　思考著野蠻的幽靈

思想者的高度　不是
在泰山只看到日出和黃土地
思想者的高度　也不是
只看到海洋和綠色森林的阿爾卑斯
思想者站在珠穆朗瑪峰
俯覽著整個人類的文明與蠻橫

啊　思想者　在茫茫長夜
我多想看到你發光的羽翼
當你飛翔在天際時
我多想乘上你隱形的翅膀

Thinker's Invisible Wings

Thoughts are thinker's invisible wings.
Anything but thought can be snatched
away, given up or forgotten, because
it's for thinking that a thinker lives.

A thinker must think for the love
of mankind without self-pity:
marching on the front line
in the war of civilization against barbarity
and democracy against tyranny,
and finding answers to the ends
of heaven and earth, and life and death.

And he must think spring in the dead of winter,
cold snap in the warmth of spring day,
dawn in the dead of night, dark shadow under
the sun, civilization in the corner of barbarity,
and ghost of dictatorship in a civilized society.

And his viewpoint is not at Mt. Tai where sunrise
and yellow earth are the sceneries, nor is Alps
where ocean and green forests can be seen.
He has to stand on the top of Mt. Everest
to observe various civilizations of mankind.

O! thinker,
I pine for seeing your glittering wings
in the long dark night, and climbing
on your invisible wings to fly with you.

是時候了

是時候了
難道還有什麼幻想不能放棄
只要邪惡中共還把持著母親的土地
就不要指望會有公平和正義

是時候了
難道還有什麼沒有看清
它公然製造著一樁樁陽光下的罪惡
卻冠以人民的名義

是時候了
難道還看不出它在大肆收刮民膏民脂
窮凶極惡地掠奪母親的財富
哪裡還把公民放在眼裡

是時候了
邪惡中共的氣數已盡
熱血已沸騰正義的火焰已經燃起
我們要奪回母親的土地

是時候了
為了公平和正義

Time Long Overdue

Time long overdue:
Is there any fantasy that cannot be given up?
So long as the evil CCP still controls the mother's land
there's no fairness nor justice

Time long overdue:
Is there anything else that's unseen?
It's committed, blatantly under the sun
innumerable crimes, in the name of the people

Time long overdue:
It endlessly drains the people's blood, sweat and tears
and viciously robs the mother's wealth
How can it serve the people?

Time long overdue:
The evil CCP has now run out of luck
The torch of fairness and justice has been ignited
and the mother's land we must take back

Time long overdue
to act for fairness and justice!

「真善忍」之感悟

真 — 真人得道以升天
真心　真意　真誠　真情
至真求真理
在謊言的沙漠上播種真理
真理的種子就會將沙漠變成綠洲
將真理的火種撒向黑暗
黑暗就會被點燃

善 — 上善若水　柔愛之心
善舉　善心　善良　善意
至善做善人
污泥中之純潔凌波仙子
蓮花的芳香會驅除汙穢
將善的福音播向塵世
塵埃會被盪滌乾淨

忍 — 心上一把刀　能之最
忍耐　忍讓　忍辱　忍受
容天下難容之人
忍天下難忍之事
忍　絕不是迴避逃離 —
是可忍　孰不可忍
該出手時就出手
與愛同行　與正義同舟

至真　至善　至忍 — 至美
上帝是永恆的美
無法用言辭形容之美
真善忍　為人之道　為人之本
真善忍　人性之美　至美之人性
唯真善忍可拯救人類
唯真善忍可帶來光明之明天

Ode to "Truthfulness - Compassion - Forbearance"

Truthfulness includes
"honesty, veracity, sincerity, no deceit, trustworthiness
genuineness, candidness, frankness, openness, forthrightness"
Be true to always seek the truth
speak the truth, the whole truth and nothing but the truth
Once the truth is sown on the desert of lies
the seeds of truth will turn it into an oasis
Once the kindling of truth is sprinkled into the darkness
the darkness will burn out in seconds

Compassion includes
"kindness, big-hearted, goodwill, benignity, benevolence
thoughtfulness, decency, public-spirited, social conscience
consideration, charity, altruism, humanity, philanthropy, goodness"
Be kind to be a good person
The lotus flower rises from the sludge of water
and its aromatic fragrance expels the foul odour
When the seeds of kindness are sprinkled into the earth
the wasteland of humanity will become the fertile land
of conscience

Forbearance includes
"tolerance, patience, resignation, fortitude, stoicism, endurance
long-suffering, leniency, clemency, indulgence"
Be tolerant to those hard to be tolerated
To endure those hard to be bearable
Yet one should not run away from challenges:
When devil attacks one should fight back
and must always seek justice with a loving heart

To the limit of truthfulness - compassion - forbearance
is to stretch our hands to the Beauty, and the eternal Beauty
the eternal God that we cannot describe Him in words
The truthfulness - compassion - forbearance
is what a human should be a human, the beauty of humanity
the only salvation of our own living universe
and the only hope to have a bright future for all of us

為什麼問為什麼

二千多年前屈原留下了「天問」
一千多年後蘇東坡依然「把酒問青天」
幼童總會問太陽為什麼從東方上昇
月亮的形狀總是新滿虧盈、變化不停

「地平」「地圓」「天圓地方」還是「地心」
到有限範圍內的「日心說」，人類依然
想知道宇宙的中心到底在哪裏。依然惆悵
人類求索真理之路是多麼黑暗、彎曲、漫長

雖然今天的人可以飛出地球、登上月亮
知道了電子的速度、光子的「波粒二相」
但無法解釋為何月亮的另一面永遠不讓我們觀望、
直徑與距離之比的完美從月球對地球對太陽

流傳了幾千年的神話「盤古開天闢地」
「女媧補天」「后羿射日」後人類樂業安居
亞當與夏娃在伊甸園裏偷食禁果
今天的人類依然詰問人類的源頭

親愛的朋友你從哪裏來？無論東方西方
再問問自己又往哪裏去？清楚還是渺茫
人類庫存的知識越多疑問就越多
人類一直問自己到底有沒有盡頭

Why to Ask Why

QU Yuan wrote Questions to Heaven more than 2,000 years ago
1,000 and more years later, "asking the heaven
while boozing" SU Shi also had a go
Kids always ask why the sun rises from east,
and the phase of the moon is constantly changing
from new, waxing, to full, and so on

From Flat Earth, Spherical Earth, Geocentrism
or Celestial Sphere with Flat Earth
To the Heliocentric Model within a limited range,
human beings still want to know exactly where the centre
of the universe is, still brooding
What a dark, tortuous, and long is the path
of mankind in the truth seeking!

Though we can now fly off the earth and land on the moon
and have known the speed of electron
and the wave-particle duality of photon
yet we don't know why the other side
of the moon won't let us to watch on earth,
nor can explain the perfect ratio of diameter
to distance from the moon to the earth to the sun

The myth that has been passed down for thousands of years:
Pangu created the heaven and earth, Nüwa repaired the Pillars
of Heaven and Yi Shot Down Nine Suns,
so human beings can live in peace.
And in the Garden of Eden,
Adam and Eve had eaten the fruits of forbidden
The mankind today is still questioning its origin

Where are you from my dear friend?
regardless of East or West
Then ask yourself where are you going?
with a clear direction or not
The more knowledge the mankind has,
the more questions to be answered
Human beings have been asking themselves
if there is an ultimate end

Footnote:
• QU Yuan, a poet, c. 340-278 BC
• SU Shi, a poet, 1037-1101
• Pangu, Nüwa and Yi, all regarded as "creators" of the heaven and earth according to some
  ancient Chinese myths

致謝

首先感謝博大出版社能夠接受出版，尤其要感謝洪社長的抬愛。該出版社的姿瑤設計師和蘭亭編輯為本書的編排盡心盡力地付出了辛勞，本人十分感激。由於這本書裡收集的大多數的詩歌發表在「大紀元」、「希望之聲」、「看中國」和「九龍叢報」等網站，故這裡一併感謝這些網站的林芳宇、文思敏、楊天龍以及安德烈等等文學編輯們的厚愛。也誠摯地感謝我的詩友埃爾韋·德勒先生在百忙中為本書寫序。還要感謝的一位重要的人物就是我的太太，她常常是我漢譯作品的第一位讀者兼評論家。本書中所用的圖片均來自 Pixabay，感謝這些圖片的擁有者。

Acknowledgements

First of all, I'm grateful to the Broad Press Int. Co. Ltd for accepting it for publication, especially to President Hong for her liking and help. The designer Ziyao and the editor Lanting are gratefully acknowledged for their hard work in editing and shaping this book. Since most of the poems in this collection have been published on websites such as the Epoch Times (Chinese) and Sound of Hope, so I'd like to thank all the literary editors of those websites for their liking and work. I sincerely thank my poet friend Mr. Herve Deleu for writing such a poetic foreword for this book in spite of his busy schedule. An important person to thank is my wife who has often been the first reader and critic of some of my Chinese translations. The images used in this book are all from Pixabay, and I'd like to express my much appreciation to their owners.

Index of Poets ❖ 詩人索引

國家圖書館出版品預行編目 (CIP) 資料

思想者的隱形翅膀——漢英雙語詩歌 101 首
= Thinker's invisible wings : 101 Chinese-English bilingual poems /
韓亦言著譯 . -- [臺北市] : 博大國際文化有限公司 , 2023.07
320 面 ; 14.8 x 21 公分
中英對照
ISBN 978-986-97774-9-0（平裝）

813.1   112011622

思想者的隱形翅膀——漢英雙語詩歌 101 首

作者：韓亦言
編輯：黃蘭亭
美術編輯：吳姿瑤
封面設計：吳姿瑤

出版：博大國際文化有限公司
電話：886-2-2769-0599
網址：http://www.broadpressinc.com
台灣經銷商：采舍國際通路
地址：新北市中和區中山路 2 段 366 巷 10 號 3 樓
電話：886-2-82458786
傳真：886-2-82458718
華文網網路書店：http://www.book4u.com.tw
新絲路網路書店：http://www.silkbook.com
規格：14.8cm × 21cm
國際書號：ISBN 978-986-97774-9-0（平裝）
定價：新台幣 350 元
出版日期：2023 年 7 月